The Sexual Life of Savages
and Other Stories

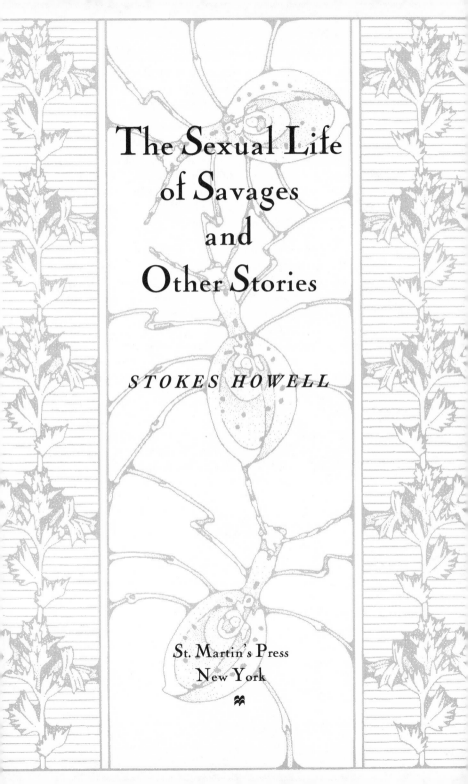

The Sexual Life of Savages and Other Stories

STOKES HOWELL

St. Martin's Press
New York

THE SEXUAL LIFE OF SAVAGES AND OTHER STORIES.
Copyright © 1996 by Stokes Howell. All rights reserved. Printed in the
United States of America. No part of this book may be used or
reproduced in any manner whatsoever without written permission
except in the case of brief quotations embodied in critical articles or
reviews. For information, address St. Martin's Press, 175 Fifth Avenue,
New York, N.Y. 10010.

These stories have been previously published: "Sin" originally appeared in
Angle of Repose, edited by Nancy Peskin (Buffalo, N.Y.: Hallwalls
Contemporary Art Center, 1986). "Legacy" (1992), "Memphis" (1992),
"Baker" (1993), "Dear Veronica" (1993), and "Achieving Equanimity" (1995)
originally appeared in *Exquisite Corpse.* "Uncle Ed" originally appeared in
Grand Street 13 (summer 1994). "Going Home" originally appeared under the
title "Mother" (1985) in *Sulfur.* "The Sexual Life of Savages" originally
appeared under the title "It's Okay" in *Tales from the Heart* 1 (summer 1994).
A portion of "My Education" originally appeared under the
title "Father" in *Z-Trem* 1 (spring 1991).

Author's note: The account of the Indian battle in "My Education"
follows closely—and Baptiste's spoken words are quoted verbatim
from—the account given in the *History of Calloway County,
Missouri,* published in 1884, author unknown.

Library of Congress Cataloging-in-Publication Data

Howell, Stokes.
    The sexual life of savages and other stories / by Stokes Howell.
        p.   cm.
    ISBN 0–312–14414–8
    1. Manners and customs—Fiction. 2. Erotic stories, American.
I. Title.
PS3558.O899S48   1996
813'.54—dc20   96–6481

First edition: June 1996

10 9 8 7 6 5 4 3 2 1

For my son Jason

Contents

Contents

Author's Foreword

This collection contains stories from two different worlds, one urban, one rural. From these two worlds come two voices, and the question of how to reconcile the polarity in a single book. The solution I've chosen here is a sequence of stories that flows from one world to the other and back again, hopefully with a progression that provokes resonances and echoes in a perhaps unexpected manner.

The two worlds: One is a small-town agricultural world in Missouri. It is here you might be confronted by a cow swollen up with the bloats and about to explode. To let the gas out you stick a pocketknife into its gut, then coax the deflated beast up a ramp into your pickup for the forty-mile dash to the slaughterhouse. There you unload it and hope the delirious animal can stagger across the threshold before it expires so you don't lose the four hundred dollars you've got invested in it. But of course these meatpackers know a diseased cow when they see one. Your investment gets cut up and gutted and thrown into the pile of offal that is marked with neon green dye, worthless hunks of rendered flesh destined for the waste wagon. You go home with no cow and no money, only to find out that the three new calves you bought last week and failed to get inoculated have died, too, of shipping fever or brucellosis or some other bovine malady you, as a novice cattle "rancher," weren't even aware existed.

The second world is an urban one, where the concrete terrain might be even more slippery than bottomland gumbo. New York City, where everyone's motor is revving in the danger zone, is a place of extremities, a place where the emotional navigation that results from an after-hours phone call from a lover who might be about to fall into bed with someone she's met in a bar, or from an urgent invitation to meet an ex-girlfriend for dinner in an Italian restaurant in Brooklyn, turns out to be not nearly as simple as loading a sick cow into a pickup and driving it to the slaughterhouse, though at the end of the night the consequences can seem just as irrefutable.

Readers read story collections in different ways and often in a different order than the one intended by the writer. Since all the pieces in the book—including the ones that aren't in conventional short story format—can stand on their own, they can be read in any order you wish.

Acknowledgments

With thanks to Shawn Colvin, Rebecca Litman, Philip Glass, Gerald Thomas, Fernanda Torres, August Kleinzahler, Monique Gardenberg, Karen Hoehn, Carole Corcoran, Larry Kenigsberg, Andrei Codrescu, Laura Rosenthal, Deborah Treisman, Rudy Wurlitzer, Lynn Davis, Lianne Halfon, Jeffrey Neale, John Moran, John and Debra Hardy, Carole Tonkinson, Ron Ridenour, Laura Fisher, Helga Augustin, Dale Worsley, Arthur Yorinks, Rachel Abramowitz, Paige Snell, Mariana Lima, Lewis Jackson, Tracy Tynan, Patricia Hluchy, Bill Schaap, my editor Jim Fitzgerald, Regan Good at St. Martin's Press, my sister Mary, my brother John, my parents John and Jean Howell, and my grandfather Roy M. Stokes. Also, in loving memory of Candy Jernigan.

The Sexual Life of Savages and Other Stories

Memphis

I met this guy who said his name was Buddy Holly at the Greyhound station in Memphis. He'd come in from Tullahoma, and I was laying over on my way to El Paso. He didn't know where he was going next. He said he'd see. I had until six o'clock to catch the Eagle, so we decided to see the town. First place we went was this strip joint across the street from the station. It was one of those places where the girls walk right up and grab hold of your cock and ask if you want to buy two beers and a table dance for fifteen dollars. How can you refuse? Buddy went with this mulatto girl over into the corner, and I had a rough-looking blonde named Angel. They had these sofas behind a partition where they could whack you off without seeming to. Angel said the owner would kick her out if he caught her, so I sat there drinking my beer while she had her hand in my pants. I felt some titty and came all over her hand and that was that. When Buddy finished we walked out and looked for a place to eat. It was only eleven in the morning. We stopped into a fake German beer garden type of joint and ordered. Buddy asked what some dish on the menu was and this beehived waitress said, "Honey, that's just a big fat weenie with sauerkraut all over it." Buddy ate that and I had some other kind of meat sandwich. By then it was noon so we walked down to the river. It was hot as blazes. We sat and watched the tugs pushing their barges up the river, watched the *Delta Queen* take a load of Japanese tourists out onto the water. We got hot. Man we got hot. We decided to take a dip. There was an island about one hundred yards out that had some kind of tourist attraction on it, so we decided to swim out to it. We got in and started across. Maybe it was the beer or that heavy German food, but Buddy just sank. He just sank. I looked back and he wasn't there. I dove down a couple of times but I didn't even know where he'd gone under and the water was muddy. He was gone, man. He was gone. There wasn't even any current there. It was just a backwater. The police said the water was forty feet deep. They found him on the bottom. I watched them haul him out with hooks, deader than hell. When I told them his name was Buddy Holly they said they'd check. He had a tattoo that said Buddy. He was 5'9", 163 pounds. No I.D. The fucker just sank.

In the Bathroom at
Joey's Restaurant

Veronica and I were having dinner in Joey's Restaurant on the waterfront in Brooklyn and I said, "I have to go to the bathroom," and when I got up to go she followed me in. She was really hysterical. She walked in right behind me and stood there crying by the wash basins. The guys would come in and walk to the urinals and look at us funny because she was hysterically crying. She was saying she wasn't going to let me disappear from her life. She had gone to see some play the night before where one character was talking about friends of his who had died of AIDS and were no longer in his life and she got panicky and couldn't sleep and called me first thing in the morning. She said, "I have to see you. I have to see you tonight." So I said, "Okay," and that I'd meet her at Joey's. Before she hung up she said, "Are you seeing someone else?" and I said, "Yes," and she said, "That really pisses me off that you're seeing someone so soon after we broke up." I said "You were the one who wanted to break up, not me," and she said, "Well I can't help how I feel and that's the way I felt then but I feel different now." We were about to have a fight on the phone so I said, "Look, let's have dinner and talk tonight," and she said, "Okay," and she said, "I love you. That's the one thing that doesn't change. I love you. I love you." We hung up and I thought, "Am I really going to have dinner with this maniac?" and the answer was "Yes, I'm going to have dinner with her."

So I went to Joey's at about nine in my new black-and-white

houndstooth sport coat from Barneys. I looked good in it, every-body said so. She wasn't there yet so I ordered a glass of wine at the bar and stared out at the river, looking at my watch every few minutes thinking about this strange phone call. Strange because she said she was in love with me. Strange because I hadn't talked to her in a month, in fact I'd stopped returning her messages: "I was walking through Grand Central and I heard someone whistling and I thought it sounded just like you when you sing the Eckankar song, and I knew it wasn't but it made me smile and think of you"; "I'm in Portobello. I came in to have a glass of wine. I'll be here for another hour or two if you want to come by. It's a beautiful evening. I miss you"; "I didn't mean it when I said it didn't mat-ter if I talked to you or not. It does matter. I don't want to not talk to you. These phone calls seem to torment you somehow and I don't want to torment you. I guess I'll just have to trust that the time will come when we can talk again. I'm sorry to be leaving all these messages. I won't call again. Good-bye."

At nine-fifteen I looked up and there she was standing in the doorway. She walked up to me smiling and when she got close enough she threw her arms around me and wouldn't let go. She wouldn't stop holding me. She was shaking. Her arms were trem-bling. She said, "I missed you so much." She said that about twenty times and kept holding onto me, and I started looking over her shoulder to see if the waiter and the bartender were taking this in. But everything seemed normal. The bartender was talking to a blond at the end of the bar and the waiter was balancing a salad and some kind of artichoke dish on his arm. It was all normal be-havior in the place except ours, but no one seemed to mind.

We got a table by the window on the water and held hands, and it was like the night after Lisa's funeral, when Veronica picked me up in her car and we drove down to the promenade by the har-bor and walked and talked looking at the lights on the water. The night after the day when the box holding Lisa's ashes was wrapped so beautifully in white fabric with bows all colors of the rainbow and set upon a stand in front of three or four hundred very sad people, sad since the day six weeks before when the idiot doctor had blurted out without any preparation, "It's cancer." He just walked in the room and said it and Lisa shot up in the bed with more vigor than she'd shown in a month and said, "What?" and the doctor started talking about the CAT scan showing tumors splashed like drops of paint across her liver. I wanted to strangle him for not waiting until Mark came back the next day to be there with her, and for having misdiagnosed her with chronic fatigue syndrome six months previously, and then hepatitis just a month before, when she turned golden yellow like a statue of the Buddha and Barry and I had to take her to the hospital because Mark was on a business trip to London. Lisa had been there a week with things not looking good before this piece of shit doctor who would retire a few months after bungling this case came in and blurted out the word *cancer*.

Veronica started telling me all the things that had happened to her since the official end of our relationship one month before. She had a new job with an international design firm that was going to take her all over the world. The preparation was hard work. It was all she did. She worked all day and went to yoga and that was all she did (she was trying to let me know she wasn't fucking anyone else). She would be going away soon for two months, then back for one month, then away for another month, then back for two weeks, then away for ten days, then back for six weeks, and on and on, not knowing it didn't matter any more to me what she did or when she did it. That's not true. It mattered too much. So much that I didn't want to know about it. I didn't want to know what she was doing or when she was doing it. If she wasn't doing it with me, I didn't want to know.

We started rehashing the events that led to the final rupture. Yes, there was more than one rupture. There was the first rupture when she said she wanted to see other people. She left, I started going out with a singer, and when she found out she freaked and started the pattern of calling me day and night and leaving those messages: "I really want you to call me. I have some things to share with you. I know you probably don't want to talk to me but I hope you'll call. Things have changed for me since Dad's operation. I just couldn't stay with you. I couldn't ask you to stand by me and support me when I wasn't sure that I could stand by you. I know this probably sounds like an excuse to you but it's the truth. I'm trying to be as honest as I can. Call me. I've left messages in all three places now, your office, your apartment, your sister's apartment. I need to talk to you. Please call me." After that first rupture, the one that occurred right before the surgery on some kind of spidery cyst on her father's brain that they've operated on a dozen times but the tentacles of this cyst just keep growing back and eventually might paralyze him completely, after that rupture came the second rupture, the rupture that was about her wanting a different kind of life than the one she had. She wasn't happy living in the city. Things were too unsettling there. She wanted a place she could call her home, a house in the country near water, a lake or the beach. She had to be near the water or she became physically distraught. She had to be able to breathe clean air and have a beautiful yard, and she wanted a dog. There was more to it than that, other things she didn't say, but these were the things she did say, so it was what I had to believe. The problem was that I didn't have a house in the country. I just had an apartment in the city not very near the water, and of course no yard and just the normal air you find in a city. She didn't want to wait around for the five or ten years it would take me to make enough money to have those things (the dog I could already afford but the house in the country near the water was something that would take some time and she didn't want to wait). So there was a second rupture and this time I went out with an actress and Veronica's friend Beth saw us kissing in front of a movie theater and that set off a whole new round of phone messages: "A few weeks ago I thought I knew that I didn't want to be with you but now I don't know that anymore. I know I do want to be with you. I was walking past your street and I missed you and I wondered why we never got a cookbook and made a dinner at home even if neither one of us can cook worth a damn. Why didn't we do that, or why didn't we just go away for a week to the Caribbean, just leave? We could have done it. We didn't think we could but we could have. We should have done something different than we did, I should have done something different and I didn't and I'm sorry. I miss you and I want to see you. Call me okay? Okay?" And then the other ruptures, too many to count, although I had often counted them and could easily give an exact number complete with dates, days of the week, and times of day and night for all of them, including the one where she told me she felt like we had Lisa's blessing and then one week later was fucking some guy in a hotel room in Ohio, calling me when she got back to tell me she was going to be seeing this fellow now. I said, "I guess we don't have Lisa's blessing any more" and she got mad and said, "I'm furious! I'm furious that you said that!" and hung up on me and called back five minutes later and said, "When I said that I just meant that I felt like Lisa would have been glad to see us together. I love you. I love you," and started crying and hung up on me again and called back again and I said, "Look, don't call me any more. I think you're an asshole" and I hung up on her. Then came weeks more of her lunatic messages: "I'm not an asshole! I'm not a piece of garbage! You didn't think I was an asshole a week ago and now just because I'm seeing someone you think I'm an asshole. Don't call me any more and don't send me any more letters that you do or do not want an answer to, don't, don't, I don't know, good-bye." And "I was calling to pick a fight with you but now I just want to talk to you. I'm out of control. If you want to talk, no, what I mean is I want to talk. Will you just call and talk to me for a minute?" And "I'm going to break up with Tom, he's a really nice guy but it's not what I want. I was up all night writing him a letter to tell him and it's the same letter I wrote to you and never mailed. It's my stuff, it's all my stuff and I have to figure out what to do about it. I quit seeing my shrink because I don't think he's what I need but as soon as I can afford it I'm going to start up again with another one. I'm sorry about all this. I'd really like to talk to you. I've never had the door slammed on me like this. I know I shouldn't call you. It was a slap in the face when you changed to an unlisted number. I'm calling you at work just because I really would like to talk to you. I hope you'll call me but if you don't I won't bother you again," and so on and so on and so on and stop it stop it stop it stop it stop it.

After an hour at Joey's I'd had enough. I wasn't sure why I came in the first place, maybe just to see what I would feel. So I said, "I don't want to do this any more" and she said, "Why?" and I couldn't believe she said, "Why?" To her it all seemed like business as usual I guess. "Because it's so unpleasant," I said. She tried to ask me about Julie and how things were going with her and I said, "I don't want to talk about it" and suddenly I felt a twinge in my left kidney and knew I'd better take a piss. I said, "I have to go to the bathroom" and she said, "Are you okay?" because I'd had a kidney stone three months before, during one of the times when we weren't seeing each other. She'd called the office and gotten my assistant to tell her where I was and then she called me at the hospital. I was on morphine with a catheter hanging out of my dick and it was wonderful, it was all I ever wanted. I was looking out the window on a cold, gray November day at the dirty East River and thinking "This is the way to live. I don't even have to get up to piss." That's how good the morphine was. The next day the doctor battered my kidney with four hundred ultrasound waves per second to break the stone up into infinitesimal fragments and I spent a day just pissing out the pieces. Since then I had been fine, just drinking water all day, quarts of it, and taking a diuretic so that in the future no compact mass of subcrystalline to radial monoclinic needles of calcium oxalate monohydrate, with microcrystalline hydroxyl apatite filling the apparent nuclear area of papillary attachment and internodular void would ever again form in my kidneys, because as good as the morphine was the withdrawal from it wasn't so good, and the pain before the morphine wasn't wonderful either. So now I just drink gallons and gallons of water all day long and stay hydrated and flush my kidneys and have to piss every hour at least, sometimes more. So I told her now that I needed to piss and that's when she followed me into the bathroom. I guess she really was worried that I was going to disappear from her life and with good reason, because I was going to disappear.

It was strange that she was in there with me. I'd never been in a men's room with a woman before. I was used to being in there with men, with the men saying the things men say in public bathrooms, things like "Hey buddy how about a courtesy flush" if someone was really stinking up the joint or "I can name that tune in one note" after a particularly loud fart. But I just went about my business. I had to piss really bad. There was no way I could hold it back. When you drink as much water as I do you don't hold anything back. After I finished she was still standing there. She wasn't giving up. She said, "What do you want to do now?" and I flashed for a minute on other nights when we had met after a rupture, after weeks or months of not seeing each other, and how great they were, how great it felt to fall back in the arms of someone you love after you've been deprived of that love and of those arms. And how she has this funny thing she does when we're making love, she gets really excited and she grabs my armpit hair and clutches onto it. It's not too painful and it gets me excited because I know it's the sign that she's about to come. And how one time she said to me, "Your sperm tastes really sweet," and how she masturbates every night in bed because otherwise she can't go to sleep. (But she didn't masturbate and she didn't sleep the night she came home to her father's house and found her father on the floor half-paralyzed from the spidery cyst.) And I thought about one of the times I saw her after one of our ruptures, a rupture that lasted three weeks, three weeks of torture, of her not calling me and my heart killing me. I thought that pain would never go away. But then she called me on a Friday afternoon and said she wanted to see me. I said, "Why?" and she said, "I'm really a wreck. My friend Carter called me yesterday, Carter who has AIDS, and he was throwing up and needed to go to the hospital so I went to take him. While I was helping him out of his apartment he threw up blood on me, then when we got to the emergency room I had to help the doctor push a tube down his nose to suction out his stomach. And while that was happening he threw up on me again and then I had to sit with him in the emergency room until ten o'clock because there wasn't a room available for him. Finally when I went home I couldn't sleep. I kept seeing his eyes rolling back in his head and having nightmares about him vomiting on me." That was Thursday night and she called me Friday afternoon and she came over and brought me a red rose, one single red rose. She came in the door with it and hugged me and kissed me and she was crying then, too, and trembling. She really was a wreck. So we lay down on the bed for a while, then she called the hospital to see if Carter had gotten into a room yet. It took forever to get the nurses' station to find out he was still in the emergency room. We went by his apartment to get him some clothes and the apartment was a mess. There was bloody vomit on the floor and in a bowl by his bed. She couldn't get near it so I cleaned it up with paper towels and dumped the bowl in the toilet. Then we went to the hospital. Carter looked a lot better than he had the night before. We sat and talked with him for an hour. He'd been reading *The Extraordinary Origins of Everyday Things* and he told us about the origins of tomatoes and potatoes. He really has an amazing memory. He told us all the details. After an hour we left and went home and I said I wanted to fool around. She started saying she didn't think it would be a good thing for us to get involved again. Meanwhile she was sitting in my kitchen naked cutting her toenails with me sitting about two feet from her and it occurred to her that maybe she shouldn't be doing that if she didn't have any intention of having sex. And I said, "Yeah, I don't see much difference between us sitting here naked talking about having sex and just having it." So we got on the bed and started fooling around and it was really erotic. She said, "I'm still not quite right. My discharge has a really strong odor. My gynecologist says the infection is gone and that it's all in my head, that I'm too focused on my vagina and I should try to forget about it." I said I didn't mind the odor and I really didn't. I even went down on her. The smell was pretty strong but it wasn't offensive. I was down there a long time. She said, "You don't know how good that feels." Then we started screwing. I raised her up by the butt and we were fucking like that for a few minutes and she winced and I said, "Are you okay?" and she said, "That really hurts, I think you hit my diaphragm and bent it backward." She felt inside her to see if it had come off and then she started crying and sobbing like she was earlier and I said, "Did I really hurt you?" She couldn't answer. Then finally she could talk and she said, "When I felt the pain I saw the image of Carter with the tube getting shoved down his nose and his eyes rolling back in his head and the bloody vomit coming out of his mouth and splashing on my face" and she started sobbing really hard. I just held her and said, "I love you. I love you." I held her for a long time and thought about the 80,000 causes of death and which would be hers and which would be mine, AIDS or cancer or a spidery cyst or something else. After a while she calmed down and finally we started moving together. I had my hand on her and she got really excited and guided me inside her and it was really good. We kept moving together and it was wonderful.

In the morning we got up and she had to go to work and we kissed on the street and it was like the first time we made love.

I thought about this in that moment in the men's room in Joey's and I felt the attraction growing, pulling me toward her. I knew I could have those feelings again if I wanted them. She was making herself available to me one more time. We could go back to her apartment in Williamsburg, to the bedroom with the soft white walls and African statuettes and Indian bedspread and the two blue candles burning by the open window. But I just stopped it. I stopped it all in my head and I said, "We're not going to do anything. I'm paying, then I'm leaving" and I walked out of the bathroom with her following me. And then she wasn't crying, she was mad. She was saying, "I can pay for it" and I didn't say anything, I just walked to the table and laid down the money and kept walking. She stopped there by the table angry and didn't follow me and I didn't look back. I just kept walking to the door. I stepped outside to the curb to a cab and got in and told the driver to take me to Manhattan. I crossed the Brooklyn Bridge and went up the FDR Drive and I could see the lights of the river and the lights on the shore and the lights at Joey's Restaurant and I watched them until I couldn't see them any more and I knew I would never go back no matter what it cost me. It had already cost me too much. I looked at the highway and saw the exit to Houston Street looming ahead. I took off my houndstooth jacket and got out at First Avenue and walked the last six blocks home, buying a paper and an ice-cream cone and reading about the weather, what it said in the paper about the heat wave that wasn't abating and about how hot and miserable it was going to be in the city the next day and the day after that and the day after that. And I thought to myself, "It's good, this weather is good." I climbed the steps to my apartment, which the air conditioner had chilled to refrigerator temperature, got under three quilts, and I was still thinking about her, wondering if she stayed at the restaurant, if the guy sitting alone at the bar who was looking at us went over to talk to her, or if one of the guys who had seen us in the bathroom had been just waiting for me to leave and if she was going to go home with one of them. That's what she said she used to do, just go home with anyone, it didn't matter who. I spent five or ten or twelve minutes thinking these things and then they must have stopped, too, because I fell asleep and didn't wake up in the night like I do sometimes. I slept all night, seven or eight hours. I woke up late in the morning, got up and called the office to check the voice mail on my telephone. No messages yet. I ate breakfast, took a shower, got dressed, then walked out into the seventh day of the heat wave. Crossing Third Avenue, I stopped to buy the morning paper. Then I descended into the inferno of the subway and went to work.

Uncle Ed

Well, it looks like the plumbing in the house is shot entirely to hell. The toilet won't flush and foul matter backs up into the bathtub. The plumber finally came and had a look at it. Now he's prowling around out in the mulberry grove over the cesspool. I don't know what he expects to find there. I let him take his own good time. Besides, there's no way to hurry him. His manner is to sit and smoke, with no regard for the glue and grease he carries about on his person. He has brown teeth. His face is grizzled. In his speech the topics of sewage and fishing prevail. It was from him I learned the two primary rules of plumbing: shit won't run uphill, and Saturday night is payday.

While he fiddled with the toilet tank he spoke to me in parables about his two jobs of the day before. He was called to a factory to clear the clogged toilets. The factory employs only women, to sew women's underclothes. "These ladies," he says, "sit on their butts all day. They don't do anything to keep their bowels moving. Turds as long as your arm." He illustrated with his own brawny forearm. "It stifles the flow," he said. "Then they called me to the school. The toilets in the home economics room were plugged up. Those girls eat candy and cookies all day. You can't imagine the turds that come out of those little girls. It's a wonder it doesn't ruin their health, give them piles, mess up their assholes. I had to go outside and take up the tile covering the sewer line. The principal came along and got hysterical when he saw a bloody napkin float by. He called the superintendent over. They both got a big kick out of it. These young girls are ashamed to show they're bleeding, so they throw the napkins in the commode instead of the trash can."

There was a long pause in which the only sound was the rustle of paper as he rolled a cigarette. He spoke as he lit up. "Mabry died last week you know. It was in the paper." I said I didn't know. He went on. "His wife took sick with lung disease. She was doing poorly at home so they put her in a sanatorium. Mabry took it hard. Drew his money out of the bank, went on a spree for three weeks, then died in his room surrounded by fifty empty whiskey bottles." "Like his pa," I said. "Yeah, Ed had the weakness, too," he said. "That's not the half of it," I said. There was another long pause. The plumber wasn't saying anything, he just sat there looking at me. He was waiting for me to start in. So I started in.

Uncle Ed was a poor shot. But that didn't stop him from hunting in the swamp with the rest of us for deer, coon, and the rare panther or bobcat. Camp was the only place he could drink in peace. Aunt Clara was a teetotaler and gave him ten kinds of hell if she caught him boozing. Camp was where he did his heavy drinking. I took a slug now and then to get the smell on my breath and act the fool, but Uncle Ed drank in earnest. During the day he was never far from a jug, and at night when he thought everyone was asleep he took drinks on the sly, getting more than his due. Tom caught him at it three nights running, but didn't say anything.

The last day out was hard on Uncle Ed. His thirst gained in desperation as the supply dwindled. Needing a deer to justify spending all that time away from home doing nothing but drinking and hunting, the rest of us fanned out to look for game. Uncle Ed volunteered to stay behind to scour the pots. That's what he said, but really he just wanted to stay close to the last remaining jug. Late in the day we came back empty-handed to find him in high spirits, bragging in his rambling alcoholic fashion about a rendezvous he may or may not have had with Mary Barnes sometime in the past twenty years. He hadn't done a thing about washing the dishes, which still lay filthy in a tub of greasy water.

The whiskey was barely holding out, but we all managed to get drunk before bedding down. When Uncle Ed staggered out of the tent for a piss, Tom replaced the whiskey jug with a jug of coal oil, hiding the booze under his gear. Half an hour later we all watched as Uncle Ed slipped from his pallet in the dark and made his way on all fours toward the jug. He pulled the cork and turned it up. An eternity of perhaps two seconds passed before he spewed and began to choke, horrible noises issuing from his throat. He stumbled outside and stuck his head full down into the tub of filthy dishwater, taking deep draughts. We had some fun out of him. He sulled up and wouldn't talk to us.

He was still sulling the next morning when we broke camp. We were almost out of the swamp on the edge of town when a deer ran right at us. Uncle Ed took his usual shaky shot and missed, but Tom brought it down with a gut shot. We looked it over. The deer was slashed and bleeding on its flanks and neck. We figured it for a scrape with a bobcat. Our bunch rode jubilantly into town with our prize, right into a large crowd in front of the bank. They went wild when they saw the gashes in the deer's hide. It was identified as the deer that moments before had jumped through the bank's plateglass window. Apparently lost and confused in the street, the bewildered animal had tried to escape into the trees reflected in the glass. It burst through into the midst of tellers and depositors and sent them fleeing in one body out the front door. Splashing blood from its wounds, the deer had then broken through the door to the president's office, where it overturned chairs and scattered the morning mail. After a quarter minute of destruction, the president managed to shout the deer out the open alley door and from there it made its escape into the swamp, where we stumbled on it.

The deer had been preceded out the alley door by Aunt Clara. She was Uncle Ed's second wife. His first wife, Flora, had borne him two children and then fell into a decline that culminated in her interment. On her deathbed she made her younger sister Clara promise to marry Uncle Ed and raise the children. Clara did it. She married Uncle Ed, raised the children, and with these actions considered herself to have fulfilled her obligation to her dead sister. As far as any other marital duties went, she displayed little interest in Uncle Ed. In fact his mere presence was enough to put her into a state of sensory stupefaction. On the other hand, certain men of the town knew her to be a high-spirited and abundantly willing woman. And indeed it was while in the company of the bank president and while enjoying his usurious embraces that the two had been surprised in a state of undress by the panicked deer. As the deer stormed around the office Aunt Clara flew out the back door, pausing in the alley to gather, lace, and button her displaced garments. Inside, the president could only shout at the deer and not run after it, being incommoded by having his pants down around his ankles. This happy circumstance perhaps saved his life as it restrained his natural courage and kept him from toppling flush into the deer's furious path. Aunt Clara escaped in the opposite direction from the deer, which was followed at a distance by armed citizens who paid no attention to her rapidly receding figure behind them.

In fact, of all the multitude that witnessed the drama, it was only Uncle Ed's daughter Liza, hiding behind a tree across the alley from the bank, who saw more to the event than a desperate deer, and who saw the frantic banker and her frantic stepmother thus revealed. But the sight did not long occupy Liza's thoughts, for her purpose behind the tree was too single-minded to be diverted, even by such an otherwise signal, for the time being at least. She was waiting for young Latham, the mechanic, to show up at his garage from his lunch hour, in order to ask him a question. To bolster his resolve in answering she carried a revolver in her handbag. A few months before, Liza had taken up the habit of dropping by the garage at the noon hour. Latham had been quick to notice her and to surmise, correctly, that she would be amenable to his advances. In short order, instead of going home to his mother's house for lunch, Latham brought it to work in a paper bag and passed the lunch hour with Liza barricaded from prying eyes behind a wall of machinery. But after two months of these lunches Latham's enthusiasm began to wane, and he let Liza know that on some days he was obliged to go to his sick mother at noon and prepare her meal. Latham's mother's condition worsened rapidly, and Latham now had to go home every day. When Liza objected, Latham lost all patience and told her flat out not to expect to see him at the garage any more. So this day Liza had come to await Latham's return, in order to ascertain his intentions toward her, as she believed herself several months gone with child.

Not long after Aunt Clara had disappeared down the alley, Liza was still patiently waiting behind the tree when along came the furtive figure of her brother Mabry skirting the shadows in the same direction. Mabry had spent the night with friends in a nearby town and had awakened that morning from a drunken nightmare to remember the events of the night before. Now in fear and alarm he was hurrying home to pack a bag and leave town on the afternoon train. Mabry, with a young surgeon and a farmer by the name of Gaines, had driven to the next town the previous afternoon, drinking all the way. Once arrived they continued their debauch. As night fell Gaines irritated them by trying repeatedly to get them to accompany him to the house of a woman he said he knew. Tiring of Gaines's insistence one of the company, which had grown as the night wore on, said, "To hell with Gaines. Let's cut him." This suggestion was favorably received. Gaines, anesthetized by alcohol as thoroughly as though he had been chloroformed, was laid out on a table and the surgeon, never without his bag of instruments, cut off his balls. It was a superlative demonstration of the surgeon's art, and his care extended to properly dressing the wound before leaving Gaines to fend for himself. It was with this scene in mind that young Mabry, waking up in a strange house in a strange town, with neither Gaines or the surgeon in evidence, fled home. Fearing recognition he passed through the alleys. The commotion over the deer that reached him from the street only added to his apprehension, thinking it the tumult of a lynching party fired by the news of the outrage done to Gaines.

"I fished with Gaines," the plumber said. "Hogging catfish. Gaines got down in the water and felt along the bank for a hole. When he found one he stuck his arm in. Sometimes he flushed a moccasin, sometimes an alligator snapper the size of a shoat. He lost a finger to a snapper. When he got hold of a catfish he rammed his hands into its gills and yanked it out. It cut his wrists to ribbons with the spurs on its head, thrashing from side to side like a fiend. But Gaines held on and hogged it to the shallow water where we all jumped on. We did some telephoning, too. Just hook up a couple of screens to the wires of a hand-cranked generator, then drag the screens through the water and crank it up. The fish float right to you. Big mothers, too. They run sixty pounds and more." The plumber and I stared at the floor, thinking about the big fish. When it looked like he had had his say, I went on.

Uncle Ed, still sore about the coal oil and his missed shot at the deer, headed home for a drink. The carnival atmosphere of the crowd at the bank had only fanned his ill-temper. Since he couldn't keep any booze in his house he hid the stuff outside, with bottles stashed in the shrubbery, in hollow trees, and beneath the planks of the barn floor, where he also stashed the empties. His mania for burial extended to his life savings, which he had interred near a stump in the yard, not trusting banks. On winter days Uncle Ed sat in a soft chair in the front room by the window, a quilt over his legs and a pipe in his mouth, watching the spot over his money with enormous satisfaction.

Aunt Clara, in the kitchen, leaning against the back door out of breath with her head buzzing, had a great shock at the sight of Uncle Ed entering the barn. She hadn't expected him back until late in the afternoon. She ran into the bathroom and closed the door, congratulating herself as she pinned up her hair in front of the mirror on her record of successful accomplishment in her romantic intrigues. True, Uncle Ed once nearly caught her in the garden with the milkman, a sturdy lad who supplied her with milk at no charge in return for her favors, an arrangement that allowed Aunt Clara to keep for herself the money tightfisted Uncle Ed gave her for the dairy bill. She and the young man were in the garden one night, as was their custom, and Uncle Ed was in the barn, where Aunt Clara believed him to be working at restoring the junk furniture he had filled it with. In reality he was getting drunk on moonshine in the back room, lit by a single bulb. Around that time people were going blind from drinking moonshine. Uncle Ed had the habit of closing his eyes when he drank, and the town's electrical system had this peculiarity, that at times the entire system would flicker out to blackness for a few seconds. As Uncle Ed tilted up the jug the lights went off, and when he opened his eyes there was utter darkness. Screaming, "I'm going blind!" he stampeded through the barn and burst into the yard, where he discovered he could see again. At the outburst from the barn the milkman fled unseen through the hedge like a singed dog. Aunt Clara put herself right and ran to Uncle Ed, who mumbled a story about shellac in his eyes and went to the pump to wash it out, too rattled even to wonder what Aunt Clara was doing in the garden at that time of night. Later on, when Aunt Clara managed to snare the banker and his largesse, the milkman was dropped flat.

Aunt Clara's pride in her resourcefulness, lending a positive glow to her face for the moment, would have turned into snarling contempt had she been able to see the dog-like posture of Uncle Ed as he groveled and clawed among the empties for a full bottle, so great was her scorn for the stuff and its users. I had had personal experience of her vehemence on that subject. Before Liza had taken to hanging around with Latham I used to call on her. Aunt Clara saw me as a likely catch and invited me often to dinner. The affair was getting serious. One Saturday night I went with some other fellows for an excursion on the river. I got liquored up and began to monkey around with the two daughters of the bartender. The three of us promenaded the upper deck arm in arm, singing drunken ballads. Suddenly a lurch threw the lot of us backward into the lap of a seated woman who proved to be Aunt Clara, sitting with a gentleman I didn't recognize. I got no more dinner invitations and was barred from the premises. Then I was gone for a while visiting relatives in another town. When I came back there was talk around town about Liza's bizarre behavior. One day on Main Street in full view of everybody she started tearing off her clothes and flopped all over the sidewalk before collapsing in an hysterical spasm. Neighbors had to help the poor girl get home.

As Mabry arrived home he was relieved to find the yard deserted, as he wanted no witnesses when he dug up his father's money. It offered a balm to his fever. Still, he hesitated in the bushes, a caution duly advised by the memory of his father's violent punishments. Within the month he had felt the sting of the whip. It was the job of Mabry and the hired boy to salt the cows and in general to look after the livestock. Through their negligence two of the animals got loose in the yard, and one of these ran off and was lost. The boys were soundly flogged then sent to fill the saltboxes in the pasture. Smarting from the lash, Mabry took it into his head to pour a layer of salt over a fresh pile of steaming manure in the yard, covering it perfectly, like white frosting on a cake. The two boys hid behind the trough and waited. Uncle Ed, checking to see if his orders were being carried out, spotted the white mound and went to investigate. Coming near enough to see that the boys had spilled what appeared to be an expensive amount of salt on the ground, he went to the barn and returned with a sack. Muttering "Those wasteful boys" he bent to collect the salt, thrusting both hands deep into the pile. When at last he caught up with the fleeing pranksters he beat them nearly unconscious.

"I fished with Mabry, too," said the plumber. "Pleasant fellow, but just simply worthless. We had a party on the river, a bunch of us men batching it. Drank moonshine and played cards for a couple of days. We took turns fetching the whiskey from a wooden vat hidden in the bushes. When Mabry went to fill the jug he found a fat old sow up on her hind legs drinking out of the vat. Her whole snout and face were down in it. Mabry had just gotten two false teeth to replace the ones his father knocked out. Well sir, he ran to the river and puked those new teeth into the water. Lost 'em. Talley was out there with us, too. His wife had kicked him out of the house for a while. He'd gone to the city on business and visited a whorehouse for good measure. Back home screwing his wife, with her just lying there dead still the whole time, he asked her to wiggle some. She said, 'Now I know where you've been!' and threw him out. Made him suffer for it."

In the barn Uncle Ed finally held in his hand the object of his search, a pint bottle holding perhaps two swallows of clear liquid, found after desperate burrowing under a pile of kindling. As he raised the bottle to his mouth he paused in contemplation of the image of his own father, who on a hunt had raised a jug to the full moon, killed the contents, then cast the empty jug into the weeds, never to take another drink. "You don't have the guts to quit," were his words to Uncle Ed.

In the house Aunt Clara tried to reconstruct the scene of her getaway, to determine whether anyone could have seen her leaving the bank, and whether the banker had been injured or perhaps even knocked unconscious and discovered in his shorts. Fearful of being connected in any way with the affair, she decided to wait until later in the day to go innocently to town to make her inquiries.

Liza's inquiry had already begun. Seeing Latham return and enter the garage, she followed him inside. "I've come for my answer," she said. "What answer?" responded Latham. Upon being informed that she wanted to know whether he was going to marry her, Latham answered, "No." Hardly had the words left his lips when Liza pulled the pistol from her bag and fired two shots into his body. Latham slumped to the floor. Liza turned and left, leaving the door open behind her, and walked unhurriedly toward home. In the yard she walked past Mabry, who was digging frantically with a stick next to a stump. He looked up for an instant into the unseeing blankness of her features, then resumed digging the fourth hole he had tried.

Liza went into the barn. She walked in on Uncle Ed as he licked the final drops from the lip of the bottle. She spoke. "I shot Latham. I saw Clara buck naked in the bank with Mr. Barrett. Mabry is digging up your money." Uncle Ed asked her to repeat what she had said and she did. Jolted from his stupor he snatched the pistol still in her hand and ran outside. He fired a shot that buried itself in the stump after grazing Mabry on the temple, prostrating him for the moment. At the report Aunt Clara ran out on the veranda.

Seeing Uncle Ed with the gun she ran shrieking back inside the house, with Uncle Ed in lumbering pursuit. They chased through the rooms, he shouting abominations at every turn and finally firing at her a single shot. She fell. He ran back outside but Mabry was nowhere in sight. Finding the empty holes and his money gone, Uncle Ed sat down on the stump and put the pistol to his head. It discharged against his skull. Liza stood still at the door of the barn, and was there waiting when the sheriff and neighbors arrived, drawn by the shots.

For a long time the plumber didn't say anything. Then he put his roll of tobacco in a pocket in his stained trousers, said, "I guess I didn't hear it that way," and traipsed out to the mulberry grove. Who cares what way he heard it. People around here will tell you anything even if they don't know what the hell they're talking about. I guess he thinks he know something, but he's full of it. He's not even related to any of them. And none of this ever came out in court, because there wasn't a trial. Latham recovered and Liza went to the madhouse, so no charges came from the shooting. Aunt Clara, revived from her fainting spell, shed no light on the cause of Uncle Ed's attack on her, other than to tearfully suggest that such outbursts are common among those who partake of the devil's brew. The small caliber bullet only scratched Uncle Ed's sodden cranium, its ricochet leaving no more than a flesh wound and a legacy of morose days. Mabry did not return to these parts, settling further west, though likely nothing would have been done to him, for the accused surgeon produced the best citizens to buttress his alibi, and charges were never preferred in the case. The sole fatality was the banker, who was much shaken by the affair, and whom it pleased Providence to carry off by a hemorrhoidal colic. Aunt Clara's grief was muted by the soothing though less remunerative attentions of the local embalmer. As for Gaines, he put on a little weight and said he'd never felt better in his life. And that the "Inhuman Operation" performed on him that the newspapers were full of had in no way interfered in his dealings with the women. I do not doubt him.

The Sexual Life of Savages

. . . go ahead find someone who'll run your life for you move to the country get the fuck out of my life yeah that's it get the "fuck" out take your infected pussy and fill it with Samoan men Moroccan men European men South American men you said you feel so fortunate to have me in your life well start feeling unfortunate because I'm out of here I'm going to fuck Teresa or Sandy or whoever else I want because I want someone who loves me not just themselves you're so self-centered it makes me sick you think that there is someone who is going to save you but it's just your own fantasy you're in love with I hate you I hate you do you understand that I hate your guts your cunt your asshole which I have fucked on numerous occasions and am just sorry I didn't shoot my load in it you're afraid of AIDS well I'm HIV negative no way I have it maybe you but not me

"What are you doing?"

"Writing a story about how much I love you."

"Can I read it?"

"Yeah. I'll show it to you later."

"Good. I'm at Alison's. We're going to a movie. I'll call you when it's over."

"Okay. Bye."

I love you I love you I want to lick your asshole again I loved it your asshole is so young and taut mine is old and wrinkly we have a date next week to take flagyl together to get rid of the infection in your vagina we'll make love then twice three times I'll work on my stories I'll get the book together I'll find an editor I'll quit the research job I'm sick of it it bores me I've lost a lot of time I'm forty it's time to get it done seventeen hours in bed last weekend fucking eating your pussy giving hand jobs busting the end out of the rubber it left a wet slick on the sheets I dug in your pussy for the reservoir tip you were flooded with sperm it gushed out we were fucking like maniacs you tried to describe your orgasm it was like the solar system you said it came down to one tiny spot like a megaphone tapering from vastness to one specific place

"Hi. We're at a restaurant having a glass of wine. We ran into Jack at the movie and talked to him for a few minutes."

"How's he doing?"

"He's okay. He's shooting a movie on Long Island."

"Well, I'm just here writing. Come on over when you're done."

"It might be late."

"That's okay. I'll be up."

"I'll call you in a little while."

"Okay."

Jack he's the bastard she almost fucked a couple of months ago how did he wind up at the movie it can't be an accident "ran into" my ass back in June she had dinner with him she needed a cameraman for the film she said she didn't like him she had to really pump him just to get him to talk but she wound up at his apartment at midnight chasing glasses of wine with shots of bourbon then she left and came to my place it scared her she said to see that she wanted to sleep with him "but I wouldn't do that to you" she said thanks for the sentiment you wouldn't do that to me but you would think about doing it to me so you might think about it again and the next time you might think you would do it to me why'd she tell me she saw him did he go to the restaurant with them what's the name of that place Casa something she didn't even tell me the whole name I wonder if Alison is even there with her of course she's not what am I an idiot she made it sound so innocent why'd she even tell me she must want me to come over there and kick this guy's balls up into his throat Casa Casa de Espana Casa Di Pre that must be it it's in the Village 743-2029 261 W. 4th I'll give it another half hour wait until she calls I'll see what she's capable of she better call back pretty soon that's all I can say

"Hi. We're waiting for dessert."

"When are you coming over?"

"I don't know. I'm not ready to leave."

"Where's Alison?"

"She's here. She called Jerry and told him she would be staying, too. It might be two o'clock. Maybe I should just go home when we leave here."

"No. Come here."

"It could be really late. That's how these nights are."

"Is Jack with you?"

"No. We only saw him at the movie."

"Are you sure?"

"Yes, I'm sure."

"Okay. Just come here when you're done."

"Are you all right? You sound a little peeved."

"I'm fine. I just want to see you. Come here when you leave."

"I'll call in an hour."

"Okay."

fuck you fuck off what's so fascinating about having drinks with Alison until two in the morning is she one of the three women you said you had slept with two of them were friends you said you got drunk with them and wound up in bed the other was a real lesbian that wasn't as much fun you said you don't have that many friends you ate Alison's pussy is that it are you going to do it again you better call and you better come over or that's it you said "take the phone off the hook if you go to sleep" no way I'm going to see if you call if not go to hell go to hell you said you never want me to not be a part of your life you can't imagine it we'll always be friends think again we won't be friends I won't be part of your life what makes you think your life is so fascinating that I want to be a part of it no one else has stayed around out of all the guys you've fucked they all got out and I'm getting out too but I'm not quite done with you yet give me three more months and I'll be so bored I'll scream bored with your arguments with your family bored with your midnight phone calls bored with your mind that can never quite understand the deepest part of anything three months more that's all I want out of this now and in the meantime I'll start calling Teresa again see if she's out of her marriage yet or Sandy she'll come running over here and fuck me in a minute all it takes is a call I might even fuck her before the month is out then I can tell you about it when I split see how you like that

"Hi. I'm drunk."

"Where are you?"

"At Alison's. We're having a nightcap."

"It's two-thirty."

"I know. I'm thinking I'll sleep over here."

"I want you to come here."

"But it's so late."

"I know it's late. Come over."

"Aren't you going to sleep?"

"Not till you get here."

"I need a little time to clear my head."

"How much time?"

"Half an hour. Forty-five minutes."

"Come over in forty-five minutes."

"Will you be up?"

"I'm up now, I'll be up then."

"I'll call you in half an hour."

"Good-bye."

what kind of fucking fool am I am I just going to sit here and listen to this shit am I that fucked up over this little dark-eyed girl Christ I've forgotten women ten times better than her it's gotten so it's fucking up my stomach how did that happen when did I start whimpering like a schoolboy just so I could get laid it's hell I'm in hell is it the wailing hell the loud wailing hell the hot hell the intensely hot hell the bursting blister hell the achoo hell the unceasing torment hell or just the swamp of excrement who the hell knows I'm sitting here waiting for her to call when I should be telling her to get the fuck over here or else we create our own hells it's true it's true but I've had a lot of help creating this one but how could I know when I met her she seemed so friendly so kind so concerned for my welfare is there anything I can do for you she said I remembered that I remembered it I was ready for someone to do something for me she did it too right from the start humping my hand while we stood up against the door of her car by the promenade cabs turning around letting people out while we did this writhing dance against the side of her car what a night the wind the lights on the water her breast under my fingers and it's come to this this pit of fiery ash this plain of razors this black line hell holy Buddha get me out of here give me some light get this hungry spirit out of my head send her back to the guy in Venezuela who ditched her men are assholes she said that the first night with my hand on her breast that guy was the king of assholes got her to move all the way to Venezuela then ditched her I guess he got tired of her pussy of her bitching of her telling him he had the wrong attitude the wrong eating habits the wrong friends what am I doing I'm taking all this just to be able to spread her cunt lips Christ on a pony find someone else to bang your ballocks against you can't be that hard up okay that's it it's three-thirty she hasn't called fuck her fuck her it's finished it's over kaput thank god thank fucking god

"I'm drunk. I'm sorry."

"It's okay. Come in."

"Is it okay? I'm really drunk."

"It's okay. Come in."

"I'm sorry. I can leave."

"Just come in. Sit on the bed. Take your shoes off. Lie down. It's all right. It's all right. It's okay."

Sin

When I was still just a pup I used to work in a store for my cousins Sam and Al Bryce. The two of them had been in business together for years, selling clothes, hardware, food, you name it. And as long as Al was living they made money, because Al knew how to treat people. If some roughshod farmer or trapper came to town, Al would take him across the street to the saloon, buy him a drink, and make a customer out of him. Al got along with everybody. He would even take time out from doing the books to chat with Mrs. Henney, a kleptomaniac who had been barred from most of the other stores in town. Her actual crimes were very minor, the theft of red fingernail polish seeming to be the obsession with the most stubborn hold on her psyche. Al let her roam the aisles freely. Once she had the polish safely stolen and tucked away in her purse he came out of his office and engaged her in prolonged horticultural conversations, because for all of her irregularities Mrs. Henney knew how to grow vegetables. Her tomatoes and cucumbers were annual prizewinners. And she always paid for her seed and trowels.

But Al got kicked in the stomach by a horse. It boogered him up good. He had to quit the business, and then he died. Sam tried to run it by himself, but he just wasn't cut out for the retail business. He was an odd duck. He didn't know how to talk to people. He made the customers so uncomfortable that more and more of them gradually just stopped trading at the store. Before long business got so bad Sam couldn't afford to pay the help, and he let everyone go but me. He fired Hugh Bates, which wasn't much of a loss, because most of the time all Hugh did was sit in the back tinkering with bits of wire and metal he called his inventions. But when Sam let Mrs. Diggs go it cost us a lot of our remaining customers. She had worked at the store since the beginning.

The roof really fell in on Sam when the finance company called in his ten thousand dollar loan. He begged them to extend it for another five years. He told them how he had invested the money in a piece of land and had counted on making a killing. Instead his plans came to grief, each year heaping fresh disaster on the disaster of the year before. First there was a deluge that carried off half the crop and rotted the rest. Then came a drought that scorched the plants down to the nub until the very stalk withered and vaporized. Finally there was the inexorable march of the army worm, which completely devoured the row crops, leaving in its wake fields infested with pigweed and spurge. Each year the prospects of a fine crop were dashed, and he ended by plowing under the scalded remains or hauling the rotten vegetation off to dry and burn. His livestock fared no better. The calves died eating bitterweed, the cows got the bangs, and the bull's pecker broke. Sam was left holding the bag on a piece of ground noted only for its luxuriant growth of noxious weeds, the burdock in particular being very rank.

Sam didn't bother to tell the finance company about the money he had blown on worthless oil schemes, or his plunges into phantom gold mine stocks, but the effect of these reckless ventures was visible at his home. The paint hung off his house in long strips, the front porch was rotted through in places, and some suggested that a thorough search of the prairie that passed for his lawn might turn up the missing Harris infant. The cellar door was nailed shut because the locksmith demanded cash in advance to repair the lock. In winter it was an inconvenience having to load in coal through the bedroom window, then wheelbarrow it to a chute down the cellar steps to the furnace hopper.

Sam was up against it. He said if he was to be hung he couldn't pay off all he owed. It was a fortunate thing that his aged mother was in no condition to be aware of the deterioration in their living quarters. She sat daily in the sunroom with the blinds pulled down, waiting for the members of her bridge club to arrive, though by then all of them were dead except for Miss Lucie, who was in a coma. With her white hair, black gown, and dark blue cataract glasses she looked like a shriveled-up mantis, and lived like one, too, subsisting for the most part on biscuits and quinine water. In the corner of the room the playing cards and scorepads lay ready on a table. She always talked about the great flood when she and Miss Lucie rode out in a carriage to see the water lapping at the edge of town and watched the bloated bodies of drowned livestock float by in the current. The corpse of a horse got lodged in the branches of a submerged tree so that when the waters receded it was stuck fifteen feet above the ground. Men had to set fire to the tree and pull it down to burn off the pestilence.

But to Sam's wife, Ethel, the disgraceful fallen state of their finances had a more ominous significance. For her it represented nothing less than a judgment from the Lord on a hidden sin in their lives. God had discovered it, and now he was punishing them for it. This was a notion she had absorbed from our preacher, Reverend Snyder, who was a fanatic on the subject of sin, particularly the evil of fornication. To him mankind was no better than a herd of rutting beasts who at the slightest provocation plunge themselves frantically into the black river of lust, which at other times he likened also to a disease or to a plague of vermin. He was eloquent. Ethel thought the sun rose and set in his rear end.

Finding no sin in herself of a magnitude great enough to warrant such a profound financial humiliation, Ethel turned her attention to Sam's side of the ledger, where through some revelation, possibly divine though more probably of mere human origin, she became convinced that Sam was seeing another woman. Once this idea took root in her noggin there was no shaking it. She began making surprise visits to the store four or five times a day to check up on Sam. If he wasn't there she wanted to know when he left, where he went, and with whom. More often than not I'd have to make up some lie, because if Sam saw Ethel coming down the street he'd run out the back way just to avoid facing her and her interrogations. In talking to me Sam attributed Ethel's suspicions to the fact that she was going through the change of life, which had made her batty. He said a similar thing had happened to an aunt of his, who upon reaching the climacteric developed a persecution complex and changed from a kind, proper gentlewoman into a wild-eyed harridan who spread terror and insults wherever she went. After about a year and a half of this behavior she returned to being her normal self.

Personally, I didn't much care if Sam was frigging the entire Ladies Auxiliary of the church. It was no sweat off my balls. But it pissed me off that I was the one to have to cover up for him. That was bad enough, but even worse was that before long Ethel started zeroing in on me with this sin, evil, and lust folderol, as if I, too, was somehow involved in the downfall of Sam's business. As near as I could interpret Ethel's rantings on this subject, my contribution to the sum total of sins to be expiated seemed to lie in my being an habitué of the local pool hall, a place Reverend Snyder had decreed the very den of iniquity. Ethel was troubled by my impending damnation. I tried to assure her that my soul was in excellent condition, but she wouldn't have any of it. Finally, feeling that she was making no headway, and that a greater power than hers was required to save a soul still young and perhaps not yet irrevocably lost, she sent Reverend Snyder himself to speak to me.

I didn't appreciate this intervention in my affairs. So when Reverend Snyder accosted me in the dry goods section one afternoon I received him rather stonily. The store was empty. I remember that it was in the summer, a dangerous time for the soul according to Reverend Snyder. The passions that contract in the cold months expand when the days grow hot, making summer a most immoral season. Statistics prove it. Temptation lurks in every shady lane and beckoning glade, he said, shooting me an accusatory glance. I didn't know what he was getting at, but I made a mental note to pay closer attention to the landscape. Possibly I was missing out on something.

Snyder was saying that it didn't surprise him in the least that the youth of the present age were addicted to dalliance, lewdness, and folly. As the cause of this ubiquitous lechery he pointed to the education given in the public schools to impressionable young minds. Why, the curriculum presented as worthy of emulation consisted of the thoughts and writings of pagans! The venerable Cicero was no more than a heathen who commended, justified, and finally practiced suicide, and warmly pleaded for fornication. His compatriot Cato was an habitual drunkard who also advocated self-murder and saw no shame in prostituting his wife to Hortensius. And the Greek (the very mention of this word was an obscenity to Reverend Snyder) Socrates, he of the fabled wisdom, was a vile sodomite addicted to incontinence and the most flagitious wickedness. Even the mathematical achievements of the ancients weren't exempt, as Reverend Snyder's probing eye discovered immoral tendencies in the fifth book of Euclid's celebrated geometry.

Then, launching himself into the matter at hand, Snyder chided me for frequenting the pool hall. The depraved young ladies found there he pronounced to be none other than the Devil's officers. The establishment itself he referred to as a blight and a sore, a magnet for scum and filth that rivaled the notorious gambling hells of Cairo in its potential for leading the innocent to moral ruin. I had no quarrel with these statements. It was precisely the potential for moral ruin that attracted me to the place. The religious proclivities of its creedless congregation were pretty evenly divided between eight-ball and draw poker, with whiskey and tobacco as sacraments. And far from wanting to be saved from the evil of fornication, I considered the commission of that sin to be the principal pursuit of my existence at that time.

Reverend Snyder droned on. I managed to bear his harangue patiently and in silence until he began shaking his bony finger in my face, warning me that souls were winging their way to Hell that very minute and that mine would be among them unless I mended my ways immediately. It was when he tried to get me to join him on his knees in the aisle next to the cheesecloth that I felt I had to say something. I ventured that insofar as I understood the business of salvation, what was required was the expression of a few Biblical verses concerning faith and the forgiveness of sins, and nothing more. And that the most incorrigible voluptuaries could obtain the saving grace even on their deathbeds by repeating the appropriate formulas, in a sincere and contrite spirit of course, that goes without saying. And if that were so, why I would make sure it was these particular incantations and no others that graced my penitent lips in my expiring moments.

This piece of impudence had a bad effect. Reverend Snyder's pious brow furrowed. His face turned red and his expression grew dark. Choking back his indignation, he first brought up the merely practical obstacles to what I proposed, namely the bullet in the back of the head, the bolt from the blue, that could terminate pitilessly and mercilessly one's life and leave no margin for last-second declarations. Then, overwhelmed by disgust, he gave me to understand in a shrill voice that the ideas I so smugly advanced constituted a heresy and could not be sustained in the face of ecclesiastical law. Furthermore, such a manner of reasoning could be and had been most satisfactorily repelled and discredited and its adherents strangled, burned, and broken with iron instruments as fomenters of schism and error. And he marveled aloud at the beneficence of God's law, which seemed to tolerate such enormities as I proposed, and indeed seemed to expect them from a source so corrupt as mere human nature, which even in its choicest specimens betrays a very censurable ignorance of His wishes. As for him, his satisfaction lay in the certain knowledge of an imminent Day of Judgment when mighty earthquakes, his personal choice for the engine of wrathful destruction, would open vast chasms in the earth, plummeting sinners like me to their foul reward, where for all eternity they would roast on the slow fires of Hell. I thanked him for his comments and told him I'd pray for him, too. Then I walked away and pretended to be busy at the other end of the aisle taking inventory of our supply of clothespins. He left.

In all truthfulness there was no need to take inventory of anything. Our business had dropped off to nothing, and the store was obviously on its last legs. This fact plus the pressure of Ethel's increasingly thorough and unpredictable surveillance acted in concert to put Sam's digestive tract in an uproar. The man's stomach was all gas and nerves. For treatment of his distress Sam was going to Doc Tipton, a booze hound and a wreck of a man who didn't really practice anymore and who had been prohibited from delivering babies after two infants he delivered died at birth of broken necks. But he still gave out medicine, and a lot of people swore by him. Doc had a sense of humor. When Lou Dekens went to him complaining that he was so deaf he couldn't hear himself fart, Doc pulled a couple of horse-sized pills out of his pocket and told Lou to take them. Lou asked if they would improve his hearing. "No," Doc said, "but they'll make you fart louder."

I went with Sam once to pick up his stomach medicine. We found Doc in his house sleeping on a filthy mattress on the floor without any sheets. Doc's pet raccoon had shit all over the place and torn all the stuffing out of the sofa. The raccoon had the run of the place. It was attached to the refrigerator door by a long string around its neck. It was Doc's last remaining pet. He used to pour liquor down its throat and get it drunk, then it would stand up on its hind legs and walk around chattering just like a little man. Doc treated animals, too, and used to keep dogs and chickens, and a goat in the basement. He had a mule named Blood that was killed when lightning struck the haystack it was feeding on. Doc regarded that mule as the noblest creature on earth. He said that pound for pound the purebred jack was the most reliable draft animal and will work until it drops. It is bred to the harness and will die in the harness. He could tell you all about the different types of mules, their uses and characteristics: the sugar mule, the railroad mule, the timber mule, the cotton mule, the levee mule, and the miner mule, which he said was always black because deep in the mines a gray or white mule resembled a ghost and frightened the other mules out of control. Doc's place was freezing. When Sam told him he couldn't keep living that way Doc said, "Why not? I'm healthier than you are."

Things were going downhill for me, too, and not just in a financial sense. In addition to losing my job, which wasn't that crucial because I figured I could get by for a while by peddling moonshine and setting pins at the bowling alley, I was worried about losing my girl. Laura hadn't spoken to me for a week because she found out that Matt Moore and I had a party at the funeral parlor with Eloise Smathers and Lita Moats, two girls whose reputations for chastity were not high. In fact, out in the cottonfields in the fall Eloise would frig you for what you had in your cottonsack. As a result her sack often weighed in at three hundred pounds by the end of the day. We had the party at the funeral parlor because Matt's father was the embalmer. The girls were a little skittish about being there, but Matt was used to being around dead bodies. He worked on old man Jenkins, whose dying request was to be buried with his wig on. He had worn one for thirty years. Only a few close friends knew it, and he didn't want to surprise the others with his bald head in the coffin. When they were laying him out Matt's father told Matt to be sure to put the wig on, it was very important. Then he left on some business in town. But the wig wouldn't stay on. The head was so slippery the wig just kept sliding off, and Matt couldn't find any glue. With the wake just minutes away, Matt took a hammer and nail and with two well-placed blows secured the wig to the skull, with just about as much emotion as a carpenter feels tacking a shingle on a roof.

We loosened the girls up with a little moonshine and got down to business. I had Lita in the chapel while Matt jazzed Eloise on the embalming table. When Laura found out she threw a fit. There was a lot of yelling. She smashed an ashtray, beat her fists against her head, tried to slap me, threatened me with a pair of fire tongs, then ran into her bedroom and collapsed on the bed sobbing. I denied everything, to no avail. Finally she calmed down, said she didn't care what I did anymore, and told me to leave.

I was miserable, and I spent a week miserably thinking about Laura and writing her name over and over again in the dust on the plow blades in the back of the store. My misery was made all the more painful by the memory of our last date, an idyllic picnic in the woods on a Sunday afternoon. Laura had packed a hamper, which I carried up the side of a ridge and down a steep ravine. It weighed a ton, and at the picnic spot I discovered why. It was crammed with enough rations to sate the hordes of Xerxes and turn them away with bellyaches, not to mention the china and silverware. I laid out the blanket and watched as Laura pulled a chicken out of the hamper, its drumsticks ornamented with ridiculous pink paper decorations. I felt embarrassed for the chicken and was glad it hadn't lived to see such a thing. There was potato salad, also with paper decorations on top. Apparently for her there was no such thing as a naked piece of food. I don't like potato salad, but I ate it and said it was delicious. She gave me another helping which I barely had time to hurl into the woods while she turned her back to open the root beer. I raved about her deviled eggs and couldn't say enough about her gherkins, which were of truly enormous size and could have served admirably as doorstops. The pièce de résistance was the apple pie, thick with fresh apples, topped by a divine crust. The crust is the yardstick by which a pie is measured, she said. The secret is in the fingers, either you have the touch with the dough or you do not. She had it. We feasted and undressed on the blanket. The sky was blue, as usual, with fleecy clouds. Later we stood on the ridge top and watched the sun go down. Laura wore a red scarf against the whipping wind.

She canceled our date to the Masonic Ball, the concluding event of the annual Masonic Fair, which included a banquet honoring the champion corn grower, a performance by Humphrey the boy orator, and entertainments by Farmer Thompson's performing geese. I had already bought the tickets so I got drunk and went by myself. I got my money's worth watching those geese. The way Thompson put them through their paces was astounding. I've never been so entertained by geese since. The fair was a great success and raised a lot of money for the upkeep of the county idiot institution, which houses our own natural abundance plus those sent to us by our neighboring county, to whom in return we send our lunatics. People here think we have the best end of the deal, from the point of view of practical utility. They say the feeble-minded can be trained to tend to livestock and perform simple farm tasks, whereas lunatics are by and large prone to purely unprofitable behavior, some of them wild and uncontrollable, others immobile and incapable even of eating their own food, much less cultivating it.

The night after the Masonic Fair I continued to dissipate my vast store of grief in alcohol, surrounded by the customary Babylonish frenzy of the pool hall. The usual girls of easy virtue hovered around the doorway, and at the curb three fellows were engaged in a contest to see who could piss the farthest. I almost got into a fight with a guy named Cade. Somehow he got sore at me and said he was going to clean my plow. I ignored him and kept on shooting pool while he was talking. Finally he took a swing at me just at the moment when I bent down to pick up the chalk. His fist hit the brick wall behind me, warping his hand for life. I felt bad about it. I don't think I meant to duck. But if he had hit me I'd have been ruined.

I had drunk a copious amount of moonshine from the pints Matt was hustling in the alley. The air inside was filled with smoke, to which I contributed the fumes from an unholy cigar someone had passed me. I smoked the thing and quickly regretted not having learned its pedigree, for it burned hot in my throat, the stub was crumbly and tasted like sawdust, and its juice was foul and bitter in the extreme. In this state of hallucination I was losing at snooker when Nell Hardin appeared before my face and whispered that Laura wanted to see me at her house later that night. I didn't need further prompting. I forfeited the match and my two bits, dropped my cuestick in the rack, and set out on the road to Laura's house.

It was about a mile out of town. When I got there the lights were still on, so I sat on the ditch bank and waited, tossing weeds into the lazy current. The full moon was directly overhead, and this no doubt was an incitement to the finny inhabitants of the stream, who attacked in sworls each bit of grass when it hit the surface. There were carp, catfish, and grinnell, and I thought I saw the black shadow of that armored cannibal the gar. A bullfrog croaked, braving death in the form of a silent waiting cottonmouth.

As I waited I remembered our first stab at coitus, in that very house, one afternoon when Laura's parents were gone. On that occasion we were somewhat hurried because out of fear, awkwardness, and sheer ignorance we dawdled so long on the preliminaries and inessentials that her parents' return was to be feared at any minute. But there was no turning back. As a precaution Laura lay crossways on the bed, and I stood next to it fully dressed with my shoes on to facilitate a leap out the window should I find it convenient to leave by that route. The floor was linoleum. We strove mightily to effect union, without success. I redoubled my efforts. She was in some pain I think. Then Fate took a hand, and in accordance with the laws of mechanics the soles of my shoes lost their grip on the slick floor, sending me hurtling forward with all my weight. That did the trick. Laura, very understandably, shrieked and dug her fingernails into my face. It wasn't much, copulatively speaking, but it was a start.

This revery was broken off by my noticing that the lights had gone out in the house. I waited a few minutes, then tiptoed across the yard past a rusting scythe and harrow. I tapped at Laura's window. There was no response. I tapped harder. The curtains parted, Laura opened the window, and I crawled in. We didn't speak while I removed her satin nightgown. In minutes I was slamming away for all I was worth. I was fired up and so was she. Her insides were jumping and squirming around my tool like a bucket full of worms. It wasn't always like that. She must have had something on her mind.

Just at this time back in town Ethel was hot on Sam's trail. Finding that Sam was not at home, not at the store, and not at the Masonic Hall, she set out through the streets looking for him. She wasn't an ideal candidate for this kind of detective work, being so tall and thin as to be recognizable from blocks away, a circumstance that had served Sam well many times before when she tried to corner him at the store, because her head could be seen bobbing down the street above all others. In her thinness Ethel took after her defunct father, who in the family photograph on the mantelpiece had the appearance of having been shoved out of existence by his mammoth wife and four mammoth younger daughters. Before Sam hit the skids these gals used to come over for the weekend on visits, and they put the whole congregation in an uproar with the outfits they wore to church. Twenty foxes, a brace of mallards, several alligators, and a sperm whale would be a conservative estimate of the wildlife slaughtered to upholster that clan. They were always judiciously seated in two separate pews, but even then you could hear the wood groan under the strain when they sat down after a hymn.

The house Ethel was headed for was Retha Taney's, as it was upon Retha that Ethel's suspicions had fastened as being Sam's paramour. She arrived at the Taney residence and began her reconnaissance. Soon, from a highly advantageous position located in the azalea bushes beneath Retha's bedroom window, Ethel could make out sounds of an undeniably amorous nature issuing from that venue. This activity could only be illicit, as Retha's husband Marshal Taney was no longer living, having died valiantly a year before in the line of duty. One morning a stranger had entered the post office. Mrs. Tuttle was standing inside the doorway collecting money for the Missionary Fund, whose project that year was the purchase of brassieres for the tribeswomen of the Congo, Reverend Snyder having deemed their naked state harmful to the progress of their faith, not to mention that of their menfolk's. When Mrs. Tuttle asked the stranger if he would care to contribute, the man answered her with curses. In a foreign accent he abused her, her forefathers and offspring, a number of charities by name, all religions without distinction, God and his minions, and the sovereign heads of several foreign governments. In parting he smashed her collection urn to the floor.

Marshal Taney was alerted and caught up with the miscreant near the ice plant. When ordered to surrender the man approached meekly with his hands up. But when he got close enough he suddenly leaped on top of Taney, and a fierce struggle ensued. In such combat Taney was at a signal disadvantage, due to his right arm having been mangled in a grain auger when he was a child. Normally this handicap didn't interfere with the performance of his duties, as witness his single-handed capture of a giant farmer who had run amuck on a train. This Goliath had destroyed the furnishings of two cars and was terrorizing the passengers, without however harming anyone, when the train arrived at the depot. Taney strode through the fleeing screaming crowd, entered the car, and within minutes emerged leading the now-docile behemoth by the hand.

But in the present struggle the powerful stranger was gaining the upper hand. Marshal Taney, an efficient and faithful public servant, a veteran terror to criminals, none more gallant nor true (these words were engraved on his headstone), shouted, "Someone shoot this bastard or he will kill me!" Unfortunately the sole citizen within earshot was Mr. Bennett, a bedridden octogenarian who could only watch from his sofa as the stranger got hold of Taney's gun, stepped back, and coolly fired two shots into the Marshal's skull.

The stranger walked away from town at a leisurely pace. Far from being in a hurry, he even stopped to fill a pipe and smoke it in front of the Smith residence. He made no effort to conceal his movements by stealing through fencerows or invading corncribs, but on the contrary kept to the marked roads and lanes, turning left when the road went left, right when it bore right. This behavior caused his sanity to be questioned. When the posse caught up with him he took refuge behind a log. A hail of bullets persuaded him to throw down his weapon and come out. When asked why he had killed the marshal he said he would explain everything at the trial. The information that in all likelihood there would be no trial did not budge him from his silence.

The town split into two camps, both in favor of the same end but proposing different means. One side, anxious to exact vengeance, favored a prompt lynching, while the other side maintained the virtue of due process and the advantages of an orderly and lawful hanging. In this they recalled the festive disposal some years back of the killer Tatum, who bludgeoned his stepmother to death with a club and smashed her children's heads open with a brick in a misguided and ultimately vain attempt to become the sole inheritor of his late father's estate. At the same time Tatum attempted to conceal the crime by running himself headfirst into a tree trunk. Having thus supplied himself with a wound, he claimed that a roving gang of cutthroats was responsible for the murders, and that it was only by a miracle that he had escaped death at their hands, too. This explanation was not widely believed. On the gallows Tatum produced another account of the events, in which he not only confessed his own guilt but went on to implicate none other than the sheriff's deputy in the crime. But there really wasn't time to consider such tardy testimony, the crowd was waiting and anxious to proceed to the picnic grounds, where punch and cookies were to be served beneath a yellow and white striped tent. Tatum was hooded and dispatched.

In the event, the group in favor of swift action won out. That night a mob gathered in front of the jail, some men rushed in, there were pistol shots. The stranger, who on account of his accent and the unpatriotic and sacrilegious statements was variously supposed to have been a spy for a foreign power or a lunatic atheist, lay weltering in his blood on his cell floor, and died without divulging his secrets.

Better for Ethel had she been one of the fainthearted who do not act upon their convictions! Better she had remained forever in the azaleas among the aphids and leafhoppers! But she could not shirk what she construed as her duty. Going around to the back door she entered the house and groped her way along its dark passageways until she found the bedroom door. In the fury of righteousness and in vindication of her sacred mission to put a stop to a defilement, save Sam's soul, and, not least, perhaps rescue his business from God's onus, she flicked on the lights triumphantly. There lay revealed, not Sam snared in the rank commission of his sins but regrettably, lamentably, the good Reverend Snyder, who was at that very second engaged in a decidedly unorthodox form of communion with the young widow. It would be difficult to say who suffered the greatest shock.

Ethel fled. For her sake, and even for Sam's sake, I wish it had been Sam there in the bed with Retha, because then Sam wouldn't have been skulking into the back door of his store doing what he was doing, which was setting fire to the place. I guess he didn't see any other way out. As his last gasp he had spent the past few weeks trying to raise money by collecting on debts customers owed the store. We went through the files and pulled out all the delinquent accounts, a staggering number of them. In fact, the idea of so much money being owed to him was a great encouragement to Sam, at least until it became evident that it was impossible to squeeze money out of those reprobates. For instance there was a pig farmer named Morgan who owed Sam a ton of money. For collateral he had signed a chattel mortgage on his hogs, these being one red brood sow, one black sow, and fourteen pigs, plus any and all increase. Payment was long past due. Sam wrote Morgan a letter bringing this to his attention: "Dear Morgan. It is a long lane that has no turning, and we feel that the turn has come. Livestock is fetching excellent prices. Now everyone has the opportunity to catch up on their obligations and we are sure you will want to be among the first to do so."

Morgan ignored this letter, and two subsequent ones. Sam wrote again: "Dear Morgan. The greatest asset any person can have is his reputation for honesty. That is a God-given blessing, but if we neglect it, and do not keep our obligations paid, it will vanish from us. Once gone, it is hard to recover, because people will not believe in you. You have not replied to our letters. You surely do not mean by that that you are no longer interested in protecting your reputation. That is what is implied when one ceases to pay any attention to notices."

But Morgan was a hard-boiled case. When he persisted in his silence Sam wrote demanding what was his by every legal and moral right: "Dear Morgan. We have written you four letters about this bill, but are not favored with a reply. We are really in earnest about this and feel that we must hear from you. The bill carries a provision that we may charge a collection fee if we are forced to take proceedings. If we have to send a man out we may well take advantage of that provision."

Finally Sam and I went to confiscate the uncooperative Morgan's livestock. We found him in his pig lot shoveling muck and told him the nature of our errand. Morgan seemed surprised and professed that nothing would please him better than to oblige us, but that he didn't have the hogs to turn over to us. The yard was overflowing with swine. "But what are those hogs I see out there?" Sam cried, with no little exasperation. "Oh," said Morgan. "Those belong to my wife. All your hogs died."

Another time Sam and I tried to seize the cattle a rogue named Skelton had put up against the purchase of harness and tools. After driving down miles of narrow dirt track we pulled up in front of a shack where Skelton sat on the porch sharpening a knife the size of a bayonet. Sam produced a sheriff's order and made a rather lengthy and unfortunate speech on the subject of fair dealing in business transactions. Skelton didn't say a word, just sat there running his thumb along the edge of his blade, which looked as if it could impale three men at once. His gaze was remote, aimed out over the trees at the edge of his paltry muddy domain that consisted of a barn, corral, and shack, none of which belonged to him but was rented from the Turley brothers. There wasn't a single cow to be seen, much less the pawing and snorting herd of fifteen head he had signed to the chattel mortgage, the reason being we learned later that he had already sold them to Tom Turley to pay the rent on the ground. When Sam finished talking, Skelton spat a stream of tobacco and addressed us. He said he had spent thirteen years in prison for stabbing a man to death, that prison wasn't such a bad place, that he wouldn't mind going back, and many more warm and nostalgic things on the subject of knives, prison, and murder. I interrupted Skelton to apologize for wasting his valuable time on such a trivial matter, reminded Sam of some urgent nonexistent business we had to attend to in town, and got the hell out.

Even as Sam was placing his hopes for a return to solvency on a gallon can of gasoline, Laura and I were occupied in fulfilling ourselves, ignoring in our throes the racket being produced by the bouncing bedsprings, until our attention was caught by a sound in the hallway. This was followed by a deep cough and racking expectoration that located Laura's father in the bathroom. After a few minutes we heard a flush, and as it died down to an interminable whisper there came the soft footfalls of doom padding their way down the hall toward Laura's door. I immediately jumped for cover to the side of the bed opposite the door and tried to wedge underneath, but the springs sat too low.

Laura's father entered the room. "I heard you tossing and turning, honey," he said. "I couldn't sleep either." Couldn't sleep! He turned on a small lamp and sat down on the side of the bed. I saw his shadow on the wall and ceiling, gigantic and hideous in its aspect, and considered surrendering myself right then, in a manly fashion, for slaughter. But I suppressed this suicidal notion in favor of the less noble yet not to be scorned attitude of cowering naked on the floor while trying to scrunch myself into as inconsequential a mass as was humanly possible.

It seemed to be working. He hadn't noticed a thing and was just sitting there talking to Laura. He asked about her schoolwork, he talked about the fair, the weather, my God the man was a veritable fount of jabbered information, running to encyclopedic proportions. Laura meanwhile didn't say a word, just yawned loudly and repeatedly, feigning sleepiness to be rid of him. I can see the scene now, even though I couldn't see it then, having my face thrust in among the lint and dustballs under the bed, as though with my head hidden the rest of me might become less visible, too.

Then he noticed the draft from the window. The room was too cool, he said, she might catch cold, and he got up to cross the room to close it. I remember the sensation of bullets piercing my heart and a wild animal panic urging me to leap to my feet, to do what I hadn't the faintest idea. Neither of these events occurred. Before he took three steps the telephone began ringing in the hall, and he went to answer it, giving me the opportunity to bolt to the closet like a jackrabbit and begin putting my clothes on. I heard him shouting, "The town is on fire!" as he lumbered upstairs to get dressed to join the other volunteer firemen. I beat him out of the house by a good five minutes and ran in the direction of town. The sky was lit by flames.

I'm sure Sam had no intention of burning down the entire town. In my estimation he meant to burn out his store, collect the insurance, and enjoy a respectable retirement. But he did his job too well, and a brisk west wind did the rest. From their modest beginning the greedy flames continued on their devouring path, licking up a small office next door and consuming to ashes the meat market and a ramshackle garage, which admittedly were eyesores of long-standing. After these appetizers the flames roared up the wall of the feed store, a two-story structure that housed grain and molting chickens on the first floor and the secret and shrouded offices of the Masons on the second, their signs and oaths lacking any power over the pagan inferno. And so it ran its course, engulfing an entire block of commerce and drinking establishments. And just when it seemed it might abate, the fire astounded the crowd with a leap across to the other side of the street. Fanned now by a breeze from the east, it began racing back the direction it came from, destroying more buildings, roasting a stable full of horseflesh, and finally ending by doubling the price of a shave overnight through its incineration of two of the three barbershops in town.

The conflagration was awesome. By the time it died out most people just stood around exhausted. I found Sam standing soot-covered and dazed, and complaining of a severe pain in his stomach. He asked me to take him to Doc Tipton's. Doc was drunk as usual. The raccoon might have been sober, but it was running madly about at the end of its tether, snarling and whimpering, made berserk by the smell of the smoke. I was afraid the little bastard was going to attack me and didn't take my eye off it while Doc prepared the injection. When Doc gave it to him, Sam sat up for a few minutes, then went into convulsions, keeled over, and died without saying a word. Doc became so blubbery and trembly that I had to call Matt's father to come fill out the death certificate.

A preacher from out of town officiated at the funeral. He did a bang-up job, too, conducting a very dignified service until Doc Tipton showed up at the church. Doc's attendance was remarkable on several accounts, not least that he had made it up the church steps in the first place. Perhaps he crawled. It was also remarkable in that Doc hadn't set foot in church for twenty years.

Since the death of his wife he had blamed God for her wasting brain fever, whose tide the specialists were spectacularly impotent to stem. Drunk and disheveled, Doc staggered down the aisle and found a seat next to a stout female relation who, in spite of the oleander-soaked handkerchief she used to dab her eyes and the heavy scent of the numerous floral displays, was jolted by a tremendous odor emanating from Doc's direction. She communicated her dismay to her husband, who brought the issue to Doc's attention. A quick inspection revealed an impressive quantity of raccoon shit plastered on the soles and sides of his shoes. And further inspection revealed he had left his footprints on the new red plush carpet clear from the vestibule almost to the pulpit. Recognizing the untenability of his situation, Doc rose and staggered back up the aisle, retracing those awful steps.

Doc refrained from following the procession to the cemetery, where during the inhumation the Masons reeled off their standard fraternal mumbo-jumbo about the All-Seeing Eye and the Moral Advantages of Geometry, tossing their obscure symbols into the hole with Sam. I don't know whether he put much stock in that stuff or not, but it's down there with him anyway. Ethel looked like she had been pole-axed, and kept that look until the end of her days. The rest of us were a pretty sorry-looking crew, too, except for Hugh Bates, who came back to town for the ceremony and cut a dandy figure in his new suit and hat, the first purchases made from the rather large sum he had received from a manufacturer in the city for one of his inventions, a one-handed flour sifter that promised to be a boon to housewives.

Before long we were attending Doc's funeral. One Sunday he and a fellow named Monk, a diminutive man with a defective brain, went into the country to drink some red-eye. Doc was too drunk to make it back to town, and Monk thought it best to deposit him inside a slaughterhouse for the night. They found him there the next morning, his legs frozen blue up to his knees. He lingered a week. His writhings with death are said to have been awful.

As for that fraud Reverend Snyder, he soon answered God's call to undertake a new work in the missionary fields of Borneo. He went off to minister to the primitive hole-men there who live on insects, snakes, and lizards and who have no intelligible language but instead squeak like bats. We heard later that he was eaten by them. If true, it was a laudable and praiseworthy act on their part. I'm sorry we didn't think of it first.

Baker

Baker has us set up to get laid. He got me drunk while he was fixing the toilet and the next thing I knew we're waiting in the Front Street Cafe for a fifteen-year-old who will screw you for seven dollars and an eighteen-year-old who was burned in a fire. Baker has fucked them both before. He prefers Ellie, the burned one. "She got burned when she was seven years old," he said. "She's had all manner of skin grafts. Her right tittie didn't grow out as big as the other because of the grafts. She doesn't like the young fellows because they make fun of her. You can have her if you don't make fun of her."

I wasn't thinking of making fun of her. She's got a pretty face. I don't care where she's burned. Baker sent her to find Darla, the fifteen-year-old. "Darla's kind of rough," he said. "I screwed her in my truck once. Ellie asked me to take her out, said Darla needed the money. I said, 'All I've got is seven dollars.' She said, 'That's enough.' So I took her out by Green Creek and laid it to her. Her nipples were dry-chapped. I don't think I screwed her very good. She just laid there chewing gum and fiddling with the knobs on the radio."

None of this bothered me. I was just drunk enough to fuck a fifteen-year-old with chapped nipples. It's the whiskey. Never drink whiskey at eleven in the morning. It'll cross your eyes. The whiskey was Baker's idea. He had old rotten-toothed Willie with him and after they unstopped the commode they were finished for the day so we drove to Carterville, bought a pint, and drank it out of paper cups. Baker kept filling my cup and saying, "You're not drinking enough." Now I'm snookered. Baker doesn't seem drunk at all. He's talking to me about squirrel hunting when he was a kid: "My pappy went over and picked up one of the squirrels I shot and showed it to me. 'You shot the sow,' he said. 'See how her workings are all swelled up in the back like a she-dog? She was what was drawing the bucks. You won't see another squirrel today.' I didn't either."

I just listened and nodded. I was a little worried. What if my ex-wife hears about this? Maybe I should have stayed in the truck. This waitress has a big mouth. She knows these girls are no good. She'd tell Glenda just to get me in trouble. I'd never hear the end of it. Glenda's already looking to nail me. She complains if I'm two days late with Danny's support payments as it is. Ah, the hell with her. She's no saint. She's been mucking around with that piss-ant Edwin Davis. I heard he bought her a refrigerator. Big fucking deal. His old man owns an appliance store. It probably didn't cost him a thing.

When I told Baker I'd never paid for pussy before he said, "If you haven't paid for it yet, you will." Seven dollars doesn't seem like much. Doesn't seem like paying for it at all. Hell, it's a bargain. I spent twenty-five taking Emily Borders out to eat and to a movie and I didn't even get my hand under her bra. She clamped down on my arm like we were back in junior high. And she's had two kids. She wants me to take her to the Cotton Carnival in Memphis at the end of the month, but that won't be happening.

This is crazy. It's twelve-thirty in the afternoon. People are sitting here eating lunch and me and Baker are sitting here with hard-ons. How does he meet these women? He's got them all over town. There's a gal named Phyllis over on the east side of the tracks he went to see last week. She's one of his steadies. He was only going to talk to her but she kept rubbing her chest against his arm while he was sitting in his truck so he went inside with her. But her kids were watching cartoons in the next room and it made him so nervous he couldn't do anything. He was afraid his wife might drive by and see his truck. She's suspicious of him already because one day in the grocery store she saw Phyllis's daughter point to Baker and tell another little girl, "That's my Grandpa." "Why did she say you're her Grandpa?" Velta asked. "Aw, she's just talking," Baker said. But Velta wasn't fooled. "You know more about this than you're telling," she said. Hell, Baker's sixty-two years old. He's seen everything. Housewives flashing their quims at him at eight o'clock in the morning. Husbands dressed in negligees. He's seen it all.

Where'd that Ellie girl go? It's been twenty minutes. Maybe she's not coming back. That's just as well as far as I'm concerned. I feel a little sick. I better eat something, some pie maybe. I'm glad we got rid of Willie. I couldn't eat and look at his rotten old teeth. His breath is awful. I made sure he didn't take a drink out of my cup. He had to go make a payment on his brother Clyde's funeral that was last month. They found Clyde dead in his house. The poor sot had a heart attack in bed and when Willie went to look for him Clyde's little Chihuahua wouldn't let Willie in the door. He could see Clyde through the bedroom window. The dogcatcher had to tranquilize Sparky so the police could get in to take the body out.

Thank God Cal Charlton didn't sit down with us. Fucking insurance salesman. He tried to sell me a homeowner's policy last week. "You need more protection," he said. Fucking-A I need more protection. More cash, too. I should have signed the papers, then burned my house down. It wouldn't be too hard. Carl Sickles'll do it for you. You go out of town, your house burns down because of faulty wiring while you're gone, and you've got the perfect alibi. It's money in the bank. Carl's never been caught. He even burned his own sister's house down and got away with it. My house is just about worth being burned down. Ceiling's caving in.

Windows leak. I thought I was going to be out another seventy bucks when the commode stopped up. But it was just a washrag. Danny must have dropped it in and not told me about it. At least we didn't have to dig up the whole sewer line again.

The pie didn't help. Neither did the coffee. It just made me more nervous. I feel like I did back when I was screwing Seth Elder's wife while he was off at a police officer's training seminar. That was a dumb-ass thing to do. If Seth'd caught me he would have killed me. I was lucky. He pulled a gun on Arlene and told her he'd shoot her unless she told him who she'd been out with, but she kept her mouth shut.

Baker was saying, "Me and Velta were up in the Dalton Wilderness. You haven't seen anything like it. Nothing but forest for as far as you can see. We'd get up at dawn and make hot coffee and slab bacon and pork and beans, Velta would fry some biscuits and eggs and it was the best eating you've ever had. It was so cold your feet ached, but that coffee warmed you up right away. I'd go to the stand and wait and come back at lunch for some stewed tomatoes and pickle relish. I had a stand in a big hickory tree. I must have fallen asleep because when I opened my eyes I saw a fourteen-point buck standing right under me. I tried to shift my gun for a shot but he heard it and was out of sight in a second."

I haven't been this drunk since the Fourth of July when I called Glenda up and tried to get her to meet me at a bar in Dawtrey. She didn't sound too happy to hear from me, but she didn't hang up on me either. There was a lot of noise in the background and she kept telling me she couldn't hear what I was saying. I'd seen her the day before coming out of the doctor's office and we'd had a conversation about her mother's operation. She was looking good. She's always looked good. Finally she said she had to go. She had company and they were ready to shoot off the fireworks. I told her I'd call her again sometime, but I never did. Now it doesn't matter anymore. It doesn't matter at all.

Oh shit, here they are. They're waving through the window. The fifteen-year-old looks like she's twenty. Maybe she is. Baker doesn't see them. He's still reminiscing about the Dalton Wilderness. Charlton's a fuck. He walked by and reminded me that my car premium is late. He grinned when he said it. He knows what we're up to. Fuck him. He wasn't grinning when he caught the clap from the carhop at the A & W a couple of months ago. His wife left him over it.

Fuck it, we're going. Baker's paying the bill. The girls are already in the truck. Baker's behind the wheel cranking the motor, I'm climbing in. We're starting to move. We're pulling away from the curb. I'm sitting next to Ellie and Darla is over by Baker with her hand on his thigh. We're on our way now. We're going. We're gone.

Dear Veronica

Dear Veronica,

What I'm writing you about is the white sweater of mine which you borrowed the last time you stayed at my house. Remember the night you got drunk and we fucked in the morning and you cried when you came and then we took turns farting in the bathtub? It's the white cotton sweater with the V-neck. I want it back. You can keep the cashmere sweater, the Peruvian bedspread, and the denim work shirt, and I'll keep the ratty white shirt with the huge pockets where your breasts would be if you were wearing it (I think I got gypped in this exchange. Three articles for one, and a lousy one at that, though I know that shirt has great sentimental value for you). But if you recall, when you asked me that morning if I had anything you could wear to work I gave you the white sweater with the stipulation that I wanted it back, because it was a Christmas gift and I hadn't had the chance to wear it yet. The other items were gifts to you and I don't want them back. The white sweater was not a gift to you. Please send it to me at work, not at home, because I don't want to have to go to the post office to pick it up. Don't include a letter with it as I do not want any news from you. That also means I would appreciate it if you would stop leaving messages on my phone machine. I don't want Lori to hear you telling me how your life is getting better and soon you will feel good enough to try to have a relationship with me again, and that your bad feelings about yourself were what was hindering you the first seven times we tried to be together and were the cause of you changing your mind every two weeks or so and saying you had to get out. I don't want to hear this myself, regardless of whether Lori is here with me or not. I am in love with Lori and very happy. She is crazy about me and she loves to go down on me, something you never were too keen on doing, though you didn't seem to mind it at all when I buried my face between your legs for half an hour at a time. I don't want to see you or hear from you. I don't care whether your mother's migraines are much better or that your father's hemorrhoid operation was a success. I don't want to know a thing. So no more messages, please. Just send me the sweater.

Yours,
Paul

P.S. I know that in the accounting of gifts I left out the gladiolus bulbs you gave me, but I consider that they don't count because they never sprouted and I had to throw them away. So send the sweater and let's call it even.

P.P.S. She takes the whole thing in her mouth and swallows, too.

My Life of Crime

Whenever I read a newspaper article about a theft or a burglary, I am reminded of my own career as a burglar and a thief which took place roughly between the ages of fifteen and seventeen, when I and some of my companions terrorized the town with our daring daylight burglaries. (Actually there were only a couple of these, and I doubt if anyone was terrorized, more like annoyed and put out and pissed off, though one woman definitely was afraid when she woke up from an afternoon nap and heard us rummaging around in her kitchen cabinets, but more about that later.)

As is the case with so many career criminals, including some of our most heartless murderers, my life of crime began with the Boy Scouts, which I and my friends had joined because the troop leader was our high school science teacher. His name was Mr. Blevins, but because of the Korean War mortar shrapnel he was still carrying around in his rear end we used to call him Old Iron Butt. (He also had a steel plate in his head, but so far as I know no nickname ever developed regarding it.) But when we got involved in scouting, the older boys told us that he was known to them simply as Butt, so we started calling him Butt too, which he didn't like too much, or rather he didn't mind it at all as long as it was at Scout meetings or on a camping trip. But one time when we went into a restaurant downtown to find him and said something like, "Butt, we need the key to the tent locker," later on at the meeting he chewed us out because he didn't want to be called that in public.

He said, "Boys, don't walk up to me in a place of business and call me Butt. That's just like calling me Shit in front of my friends." So we didn't do that anymore, and Butt wasn't the kind of man to stay mad at us, although he did get mad enough on one trip to hold Roy Randolph's head between his legs and fart on him because Roy had filled Butt's sleeping bag with fish guts from all the fish we had caught. Butt was mad, he was furious, and who could blame him? He farted on Roy's head for about half an hour and afterward Roy ran down to the shore and washed his head over and over again with the freezing cold lake water. Another time Butt got mad was when we strung one of Randy Barlow's mother's brassieres across the front of Butt's Oldsmobile and he drove it uptown with the bra attached to his bumper. He was a laughingstock for a long time after that one, but he took it pretty well. He said, "Where did you get that brassiere, off a cow?" Barlow went home and told his mother what Butt had said and she called him up and chewed him out and then Butt turned around and chewed us out too. But he got over it.

We were what were called Explorer Scouts, and that's what we did, we explored. And I think that was the main reason Mr. Blevins had taken on this position of leader, because it meant that he got to go on trips with us. We earned money during the year going door-to-door peddling glow-in-the-dark telephone dials, pen-and-pencil sets, hairbrushes, and so on, all sorts of useful and useless merchandise that people bought not so much because they absolutely had to have a glow-in-the-dark telephone dial but because we were Boy Scouts and were raising money for a good cause. Another financing scheme we hit on was to sell American flags on flagpoles to merchants and homeowners, including in the price a contract engaging us to raise the flags on the major patriotic holidays and other significant dates during the year. So our patriotism and civic-mindedness were not in doubt at all, at least in our home town, but when we went on the road we became no better than a roving pack of thieves, because what we did on these trips in addition to sightsee was shoplift. There was a competition on to see who could steal the most merchandise over the duration of the trip. On our first trip to Lake Stillwater we would walk into a store and just pick up anything, knives, combs, cigarette lighters, we were like locusts ravaging the trinket counters of these cheap tourist joints. Then we got bolder and infested the pinball emporium where the owner was fool enough to have left the keys hanging from the backs of some of his machines. We stole the keys and spent the afternoon emptying the pinball machines of their change, and I don't know why we didn't get caught, because the place wasn't that crowded and it should have been obvious who the culprits were, but no one said a thing.

Next we turned to a tavern near our campground, which was on a little spit of land on the lake with ducks and other birds around. The first day we were there Teddy Raines said if we caught a duck he'd fuck it, and we tried but couldn't catch one, and Teddy then turned to humping a knothole in a tree trunk to keep himself occupied. He was by far the horniest one there, the rest of us were more into stealing. One morning Butt found him jerking off in his tent and threw the flap open and we all came running from the campfire to see. Butt was laughing and saying that Teddy was having a date with Minnie and her four daughters. Teddy got pissed off and didn't go with us on our excursion to the tavern where we had seen a beer truck delivering its load. The beer cases were stacked inside the back door, so Barlow and I just ran up and grabbed the two top cases and then ran like hell down into the woods behind the tavern to our camp to hide the beer. We drank it that night and we even let Teddy have some. He was laughing about what had happened earlier, that's how much sense he had.

So this was the first of our alcohol thefts and when we got back home we tried it again. Barlow and I stole two cases off a Busch beer truck parked behind Williams' bar, put them in my car and drove out into the country to hide them in an old shack. We went back to town to get Mason to show him and when we got back to the shack and opened the boxes we found we had stolen two boxes of empty bottles. Mason was like a madman, he went mad, he grabbed the bottles one by one and hurled them against the walls of the house shouting "Empties! Empties!" and kept on until he had shattered all forty-eight. The next time we were careful to get actual beer, in cans, but it was two cases of cans of Stag beer, an awful beer that everyone said tastes like cow piss. We got away and hid it along a ditch bank in the high grass, but someone saw us, a guy we knew in school. The bar owners were putting pressure on him to tell but he wouldn't, so we sweated it out for a couple of weeks and were afraid to even go look at our beer. Finally we went there one afternoon and the mowers had come along to mow the ditch bank and there were our two cases with the tops sheared off and the cans destroyed, so we didn't get to drink any of that beer either.

Now we moved into high gear. We wanted whiskey and hard liquor, and as I remember it was also about this time that I was reading a book about a boy and a girl who had run away from home and were living in an abandoned boxcar and broke into houses to steal food and money. This sounded like the greatest thing on earth to me so I decided to put it into practice for myself, which only reinforces the idea that young people should be shielded from reading material that might corrupt them. It's an old idea, hundreds of years old, I recently found it in a nineteenth-century philosophy book that presented as evidence the case of a young girl who was secretly reading novels. At first her family thought nothing was unusual, only that she was quiet and withdrawn and pensive at mealtimes and always went back to her room after dinner. But gradually it became too much to ignore and they questioned her and found she had been reading novels. So they hurried her to a doctor and applied leeches and bled her and tried to restore her but it was too late, she had been totally corrupted. The writer didn't say precisely how she had been corrupted but he leads you to believe that it was self-abuse that so sapped her life forces that she was utterly incapacitated. She was reading novels and masturbating, "sinning against oneself" as the Catholics describe it, like my Irish friend who went to confess to the priest when she was fourteen that she had been sinning against herself. The priest, evidently somewhat of a libertine, told her, "Don't worry about it, I do it all the time myself." But the poor nineteenth-century masturbating girl lost her mind in spite of the doctor's and her family's best efforts. She was lost at the age of eighteen and confined the rest of her life to an insane asylum, ruined by words. That is the story as I remember it from Winslow's *Intellectual Philosophy.* Winslow himself no doubt was a bloody old wanker, seeing as how he took such glee in describing an event which probably didn't even happen but that he made up to prove his point that young people would be much better off reading his own *Intellectual Philosophy,* which might just have sold fifty copies even with counting family and friends and copies supplied to libraries, instead of corrupt and insidious trash novels. Bloody old wanker.

Probably I, too, would have been better served reading Winslow's *Intellectual Philosophy* but instead I was reading this novel about the boy and girl in the boxcar stealing. That was the life I wanted to live, so I set out one night by myself and walked around by the high school and saw a house that was dark. The porch light was on, so I went up and knocked ready to say I was on a scavenger hunt if anyone answered, but they didn't. That was at a time when people still left their doors unlocked (though the activities of my fellow Scouts and I put an end to that before long, but at this time the doors were still unlocked) and I walked in and it was a thrill to be in someone else's house with them gone, it was like kissing a girl though I still hadn't done that yet, at least not seriously. The only girlfriend I'd had was Margaret Baxter who wouldn't let me stick my tongue in her mouth, I don't know why. I'd met Margaret when she and Terry Billups and Susan Spangler had come up to the grocery store where I worked. Terry pointed to Margaret standing outside and said, "That girl is in love with you." I looked at her and she looked pretty good so I thought to myself, "Well, that's a good enough deal," so I went with them to the movies. I was nervous because I'd heard some weird things about Susan Spangler, like that she had fucked herself with a coke bottle and with a hot dog that had broken off inside her and she had to pick out the pieces with a toothpick. I was afraid because I didn't have any experience with girls and here I was thrown into the midst of what looked like a pretty sophisticated situation, and Terry was a little weird, too, though I didn't know it at the time, only years later when he got spaced out on speed and practically catatonic, but Terry was a Boy Scout so I trusted him. But I wondered about this girl Margaret and I decided because I was so scared that if we got back to Susan's house after the movie and they all started taking their clothes off I would announce that I wasn't going to hang around with a bunch of sluts and leave. But that didn't happen at all, in fact this girl Margaret was rather prudish as I said and wouldn't even kiss with her mouth open until two years later when I was drunk and wound up in the backseat of someone's car with her and she was drunk and we French-kissed for the first time and we weren't even going together then. So I went out with Margaret for a while but we ultimately broke up. Then one night she came to the Midget Baseball League concession stand after the game was over, this was another thing we Boy Scouts did to raise money for our crime sprees across the country, we sold popcorn and sodas to the Midget Leaguers and their families. And Margaret was there and Marsha Sloan and Tom Carswell who later went with her and didn't get her pregnant, it was some other guy, and Teddy Raines, the same guy who said he would fuck a duck and who actually did hump a knothole and was caught jerking off in his sleeping bag, and Teddy pissed into a bottle of Mountain Dew and gave it to Margaret to drink. Margaret almost took a drink but could tell something was wrong and poured it out instead, and if I had been going with her I guess I would have had to fight Raines for pulling a stunt like that, but I wasn't and I didn't. Then Margaret's friend Marsha said to me that Margaret thought I broke up with her because she wouldn't go to the bushes with me but now she would. But now I wasn't interested, I was more into burglary then, and I said I wouldn't break up with her because of that but really I was just saying I didn't want to be with her.

So I'm in these people's house that I intend to burglarize and I look around and first of all I check out the cabinets and I see some crème de menthe which I set out because at that time besides beer mostly I had been drinking cherry sloe gin because it was like cough syrup. This looked like green cough syrup, like NyQuil, and it didn't have to be mixed and would be easy to drink so I took it and a bottle of vermouth even though I didn't know what it was, but I was after quantity, too, and I took two more bottles four in all, and then I looked around in the bedroom and saw some men's magazines like *Argosy* and *True*. I thought this might be good whacking-off material so I took the magazines, then I saw a coin purse and opened it and found ten dollars and took that. In all it was a pretty good haul, so I left and carried the stuff to my car, which I had parked a few blocks away and took the bottles out to a lane in the country and buried them and took home the books, which were more like adventure stories than whacking-off material so that wasn't any good, but I didn't throw them away I just put them inside a drawer and put the ten dollars in my wallet and that was the start of my housebreaking career.

The next day at school I told Mason and Barlow and they didn't believe me so the next night I took them with me. We went back to the same house, how stupid can you be, and took more bottles. We just about cleaned them out, took probably fifteen bottles and buried them in the country lane and were filled with enthusiasm for this business and kept a list of our booty that we showed a couple of other of our Scout cronies, and they wanted to get in on it too. So we made plans for a big haul that weekend because we knew that the Hunt girls' parents were going out of town and the girls would stay with their grandmother and their parents were the biggest drinkers in town, they had a liquor cabinet the size of a station wagon, and that was going to be our next job. But I couldn't wait for the weekend. I wanted more action immediately, so the very next night I went to the house where our neighbors the Wheelers, who were also big drinkers, lived. The Wheelers were famous for having wild drunken parties on Saturday night, then trooping into church the next morning with massive hangovers and sunglasses and sitting in the back rows, where young people such as myself sat and cut up during church, doing things like having pencil fights and flicking boogers into the senior girls' teased-up hair. During one of these wild parties we heard a trombone playing and looked out the window and a woman who was my Sunday School teacher was riding on the back of Mr. Wheeler, riding him like a horse and playing the trombone, yelling for my father to come out and join the fun. And this was just one of my Sunday School teachers, there was another one, a man, who taught the teenagers, the two of them did it together, a man and a woman. We thought the man was pretty cool, but a bit odd, I remember hearing he could be seen sitting on the street corners late at night and behaving oddly. In our class he even talked to us about sex, saying there was more to it than the man just rolling on top of the woman and rolling off. He was much better then the other teacher we got later on who told us to raise our hands if we didn't care whether our wives were virgins or not. My cousin Kenny Post and I raised our hands and the teacher went and told my mother who questioned me about it saying, "Maxine said you didn't care if your wife is a virgin," and I said, "That's right," and my mother didn't say any more because in our household we were very reticent about sex. My brother said the only thing ever said to him was one night when our father came into his bedroom harrumphing and coughing and acting nervous and sat down, and my brother was on the bed reading and wondering what the hell it was all about and finally my father said in a kind of strangled harrumphing voice, "Has that thing between your legs been bothering you?" My brother was just about to die but he said, "No," even though he'd been beating his meat for a couple of years by then. Dad harrumphed a few more times and then got up without saying anything else and left the room and that was all that was said about the subject. And with my sister it was almost the same. She was reading in bed one night except this time it was my mother who opened the door and cracked it just enough to send a little booklet about sex sailing into the room where it landed on the bed, my sister thanking God that she didn't say anything to her. The next day when Mom asked her if she had any questions she said no. The only bit of information that came to me was one day when my mother said, "If you ask a girl to go swimming and she says she can't, don't ask her why." I don't even know what brought that up except it was summer and my mother probably had been sitting around worrying that I was going to ask a girl to go swimming and when she said no I would ask her why and create a horribly embarrassing situation for the both of us.

My Life of Crime

The Sunday School teacher who was odd and who told us about sex, his name was Jim, later killed himself, apparently he had mental problems. One day he disappeared and was missing for days and there was a search, with all the church members and law enforcement people driving up and down the country roads and going up in airplanes, and finally they spotted Jim's car parked near an abandoned quarry and went there and found him dead, he had blown his brains out with a shotgun. After that Kenny Post and I used to whisper when we were in church listening to the choir that we could hear the voice of Jim's ghost in the choir loft. No one really talked about it much, they just said he had been depressed, and I got to thinking that maybe in that Sunday School class what was really going on was not just that Jim was trying to help us, but that he was also trying to get some kind of help *from* us, and that somehow we had let him down because he had to go off and kill himself all alone out on that empty quarry road. There were other strange things going on in church at that time, too. I remember my brother coming home one Sunday and telling me he had gone into his Sunday School classroom early that morning and found Harris Porter stealing money from the collection jar, and Harris said, "Don't tell on me. Don't tell. I'll suck your dick if you don't tell." My brother said, "No you won't suck my dick either," and just walked out, but he didn't tell on him. And this kind of thing seemed to be infesting all the local organizations, there was a different Boy Scout leader we'd had when we were younger, Wilson Green, who was an exhibitionist and lived half a block away from us. My sister and her friends used to get out the binoculars and watch him stand naked in front of his window. When Larry Gilder's mother heard about it she said, "Well I'm just going to drive over there and take a look," and she did and sure enough she saw him and she couldn't believe it. But no one did anything, they just said Wilson's acting a little strange again, and I never heard that he ever bothered anyone other than just showing his thing out the window. But then there was another scoutmaster, one who came along later, who was in charge of the younger boys, and this pervert would have a different boy sleep in the tent with him at night and give them "massages." He did it to about three of my friends and they told me but we didn't think anything about it, and that scoutmaster left after a year or two and probably went on giving massages to other scout troops in other towns.

So I entered my big-drinking neighbors' house by the back door, which was unlocked and immediately their dog, a dog I knew, a big golden retriever named Charley, was there and he was growling and wagging his tail at the same time. He was confused. He knew me but he knew I wasn't supposed to be there in the dark with the family gone. But he calmed down and followed me to the liquor cabinet where I got five or six bottles and got out of the house quick and went back home. My parents were gone, maybe to the same place as the Wheelers, probably the country club, so I put the bottles in the backseat of my father's car and took them out to the stashing place and buried them, and there are probably still bottles buried out there because we never found them again after the heat was put on us and we didn't want to find them. But then again they might be broken and plowed up, because this country lane, which was where I later took Carla Craddock, the new football coach's daughter, to park, got plowed up and planted by the farmer who lived next to it, something Carla and I discovered one night when we went there to frolic around. We had gotten undressed and dressed again and were driving out down the road when we hit a huge lake where the road had been plowed and become a sinkhole where water collected. We were stuck, dead stuck, no way to move out of there. So I had to walk up to the farmhouse to call a wrecker and the farmer said we were the second ones to get stuck that night. There had been three more the night before and it was too bad, but he needed the ground for planting and was tired of people driving up and down the lane at all times of the night. He wasn't mad, just kind of amused. He said I had gotten farther down the road than any of them before getting stuck. So we called the wrecker and Ace Parker came after about half an hour and he was apologizing because there was a line of cars following him. It was a hobby of some people in town to follow a wrecker to see if there was a wreck or to see who was out parking and had gotten stuck. Ace had tried to lose them but they managed to stay with him. So I walked up to the first car and it was Perry Drake and Duncan Helt, and Perry was falling all over himself apologizing saying, "I didn't know it was you, I wouldn't have come out here, I'm sorry," like he thought I was going to beat his ass, though I'd never beaten anyone's ass in my life except maybe my cousin the time he spit milk in my face and I got mad and went home and he followed me and he should have left me alone because I was mad but he wouldn't and I got him down in the bushes and pounded on his sore arm, the one he'd gotten a shot in that morning. I made him cry and later I felt terrible about it, I wasn't the ass-kicking kind. So I told Perry it was okay and he kept apologizing and it was interesting to feel myself feared when I didn't feel like a fearsome person. But Ace got us out, and the cars went back to town and my father got the bill and I had to make up some story about a flat tire and the jack wouldn't work and getting hauled into town, and he didn't ask me what I was doing out there or if the thing between my legs was bothering me and I was glad.

Then came the night of the big haul. Four of us: Barlow, Mason, O'Brian, and I drove around town until ten o'clock, then pulled into the alley by an empty house down a few houses from the Hunts' house, which was the treasure trove of liquor in the town. I waited in the car and the three others went to the house and minutes went by, five ten fifteen and then I could hear them coming down the alley. Their arms were loaded as full as they could be and they were yelping and hollering not real loud, just kind of squealing with glee. Just then behind us car lights came sweeping across the bushes and a police car pulled into the alley behind our car and I just about shit. Barlow dropped his bottles on the ground and kicked them under the front of the car and Mason and O'Brian dropped theirs in the bushes and we stood up shaking and trembling as the police car pulled up and the cop sat there and shined his light on the vacant house and then got out and walked over toward us. We walked toward him to keep him from getting too close to the bushes with the bottles in them. He asked us what we were doing and we said we were looking for Denny Batson who we thought lived there, but the house was empty so we were just taking the opportunity to take a piss. He looked around and shone his light on the house and walked up and tried the door and looked to see if any windows were broken and we were all about to shit with our hearts pounding. He came back and said a neighbor had called from across the street and he took our names and addresses and we didn't lie because we were scared and because we figured he might know who we were anyway. It was terrifying, it was the first time I had come into contact with the police though later on it happened again, and again it involved liquor though then it was just that we were underage and drinking it, not stealing it. We were parked on a road with two other cars, Teddy Raines the would-be duck fucker was there and had just left with two girls who had been in my car and left to meet us later in town, and we had some beer, a couple of six-packs, and some whiskey and a state trooper pulled up. The other cars had just left and O'Brian and Mason and I got caught and the trooper checked the trunk and found two beers and had us follow him to the police station. He made us follow him upstairs and he took O'Brian inside to question him while Mason and I were sitting outside in the waiting room on the second floor. I was thinking about the pint of whiskey in the glove compartment and the six-pack under the front seat and thinking that so far they only had two beers on us and might let us go but if they found the hard liquor it might be a lot worse. So I asked the other cop if I could go to the bathroom and he said it was downstairs so I went and ran out a side door to the car and got the whiskey and the beer and took it and hid it in the weeds behind the police station then ran back into the building. O'Brian was still in the room, who knows what he was telling the trooper because a year later when a whole bunch of us got caught spray-painting the windows of the high school it was O'Brian's fault because he was the one who got called out of class and marched to the principal's office and turned us all in when he didn't have to. We said, "O'Brian, why did you tell on us?" and he said, "They already knew," and we knew then that the principal had outfoxed him and we were all in hot water. When the principal called me in and said, "Were you involved in this?" I said, "No," and he said, "Don't look at me like a possum eating shit," and then I said, "Well okay, you got me." And the boys all got five licks with a paddle and the girls got twenty-five-page themes because the principal didn't believe in paddling girls but he believed in paddling boys. He paddled hard. He was a former wrestler, and he made you bend over with your hands on his desk and he raised me off the floor with each blow and it hurt like hell. I tried hard to keep the tears from running out of my eyes and I had the imprint of my jeans pockets tattooed on my ass for three days. But O'Brian didn't do any damage at the police station, he held his ground, and the trooper called me in next and sent O'Brian out and he talked to me and he said, "I don't understand it, why are you boys out drinking? Why aren't you at the basketball game?" and I said, "The game is in Crawfordsville," and he said, "Why do you want to get drunk?" and I said, "I don't know, you know how it is, you just like to drink a little and feel

a little high," and he said, "I've never had a drink in my life," and
I thought, "Oh, shit, he's going to nail us to the wall, he's a teetotaler and even drives the church bus on Sunday, he's going to
let us have it." But then an old couple was brought into the station, they were horrible, the old man was slobbering and filthy
and the old woman was foul-mouthed and disheveled and the
trooper lined us three boys up to watch them being processed and
said, "How old do you think they are?" and we said, "I don't
know, sixty?" and he said, "They're both forty . . . that's what alcohol can do to your life," and O'Brian correctly saw this was the
time to do some brown-nosing and said, "Oh, that's awful, that's
terrible, I never want to be like that" and Mason and I made noises
like, "Yeah," "Ummmmh," and "Ohhhhh," to indicate that we
agreed. And I guess that impressed the trooper because he let us
off, maybe he thought he'd scared us off liquor forever but the next
morning on my way to work at the grocery store I parked my car
behind the police station and picked up my pint of whiskey and
the six-pack from the weeds and put them in the trunk and we
drank them down that very night.

But the night of the big haul the policeman didn't take us in,
he just took our names and told us to leave. We were waiting for
him to pull his car out from behind us and onto the street so his
headlights wouldn't shine on the bottles under the car as we pulled
out, and I was praying that I wouldn't run over any of the bottles
and I didn't and the cop didn't see, so we pulled out and followed
the police car for a couple of blocks and then turned off and drove
around for fifteen minutes planning and being scared because of
course someone had to go back and put those bottles back in the
house because they had our names and if anything was found missing in that neighborhood we were the obvious perpetrators. So I
dropped off O'Brian and Barlow and they walked down the alley
from the other end and I guess they put it all back in good order

because we picked them up half an hour later and no one saw them and no one not even the Hunts ever reported anything wrong or missing.

And this should have dissuaded us from continuing our life of crime but it didn't. We were driven, it was an obsession, we just wanted to steal. We didn't even drink that much, in fact I don't remember drinking any of those bottles of booze. But we came up with another plan, this time it would be the Reynolds's house, they were big drinkers, big country club members and members of the hung-over back pews at the church with dark glasses. So one Sunday afternoon when we knew they would be playing golf we decided to loot their house. We drove out in Barlow's car, he parked in the driveway and it was broad daylight but the house was on a road on the edge of town so it wasn't likely we would be spotted or so we thought, we didn't think too clearly in those days apparently. The three of us went up and knocked on the door. We had an alibi ready if anyone was home, which was that we were looking for Patsy Kreston, one of the girls whose hair we flicked boogers into at church, who baby sat for the Reynolds. We rang the doorbell. I don't know why we didn't call beforehand, I guess we figured the doorbell would do and no one answered so we walked right in this being still as I said the era of unlocked doors even though by now there must have been some serious consternation making the rounds among the country club drinking Sunday back pew set that their houses were being systematically looted of liquor. But the door was unlocked and we went in and were marveling at the quantity of liquor bottles we saw in the cupboards. There was a lot of vodka and Old Granddad and Old Crow and Old Charter and Old Taylor and Seagram's 7 and Seagram's Crown Royal, it was like King Tut's tomb! We were opening cupboards and saying, "Here's more! Here's more!" and then we heard a voice from the hall saying,

"Who is it? Who is it?" a woman's voice, and I knew it was Mrs. Reynolds, who might have skipped church that morning to sleep off a binge from the night before, but still for all that didn't deserve to have three sixteen-year-old Explorer Scouts rifling her liquor supply in the middle of a Sunday afternoon and we knew it and she knew it. As soon as we heard her voice we were hightailing it out the carport door, me trailing the two others and all three of us running for our lives. Luckily Barlow had turned the car around in the driveway so that it was facing the street and he saw us come running out of the house like madmen and he started the car rolling as soon as O'Brian and Mason got in the back. It was rolling slowly toward the street by the time I got there and the window was open so I ran and dove headfirst into the open window of the rolling car and I made it and we were off, tires spinning and gravel flying, off down the road and scared shitless. We went to my house and I changed clothes and got my car and followed Barlow to his house where he parked his car and we drove around town wondering if we had been recognized and knowing she must have seen the car and trying to determine how many cars there were in town like that one and we could only think of one.

Then began the Inquisition, when I came home late in the afternoon. My mother wouldn't come right out and ask if I had been burglarizing her friends' house that afternoon, no, we were reticent about everything in that house. So, instead of asking me was I burglarizing the Reynolds's house, she began with her indirect line of questioning like, "What did you do this afternoon?" and "Whose car were you in?" and "What were you wearing?" and I lied and lied and lied, no way was I going to confess to this. I stonewalled her and that's the way it went all that week. I stonewalled and she would say, "Emma thinks she knows who did it," and I said nothing, and she would say, "Emma says if the boys come forward she won't go to the police," and I said nothing because I knew damn well Emma wouldn't go to the police, what was she going to do, have her friend's son taken to jail? After all we went to the same church and country club and she sat in her dark glasses hung over in the pew right in front of me and her best friend Mrs. Tyler rode Mr. Wheeler's back like a horse playing the trombone yelling for my father to come join the party, so what were they going to do? Not much, only if they could get me to confess and I wouldn't, and the other boys wouldn't either, so none of our parents got anywhere with us. Later on when I was in college things didn't work out so well, my mother found a letter from Mason to me about smoking pot and she called me into the living room and said, "How deeply are you involved in this marijuana thing?" And I was scared because I had two pounds in the basement I had brought home from college in Texas. It was good dope, too, Thunderfuck it was called, it was like taking acid, it got you stoned for a long time and gave an acid rush. She said, "Do you want to be an addict?" and I had to keep my mouth shut and act serious even though I knew I wasn't going to get addicted to pot, but I was afraid she would find the pot in the basement so I told her, "I'm not an addict, I only have a little," and she said, "Bring it to me," and I brought out about three joints and she made me take them out to the trash can and burn them and that seemed to satisfy her. So that night after she and my father were asleep I went to the basement and packed the pot into baggies and put it in mayonnaise jars and sealed them with candle wax and took them outside and moved the entire woodpile and dug a hole and buried the pot and moved the woodpile back on top of it and went to bed. And it was a good thing I did because soon I found out there was a search warrant out on my parents' house, but that is enough about drugs that is another story.

Somehow I felt I would get away with the attempted burglary of the Reynolds's house and all the other crimes even though I was scared and had that burning feeling on the back of my neck, that flushed hot feeling I used to get when I got in trouble at school, like the time in first grade I got an F on an assignment where I was supposed to be making the letter *m* on a piece of paper but instead spent the time talking, so that when the teacher called for the paper I could only mark three or four huge m's on the sheet that was supposed to be filled with lots of little practice m's, and I got an F and was so ashamed I took it home and flushed it down the toilet. I was nervous and worried all that week after the Reynolds fiasco but even then I didn't stop, not yet, I felt so invulnerable that even the very night of the day we almost got caught Barlow and I went to the Henry's house, some other heavy country club drinkers though not Congregationalists but Methodists, we went there that same night and stole some liquor, that's how crazed and obsessed we were about stealing into people's homes. But that was actually our last sortie, because the week or two of inquisition was so nerve-racking it cured us of going into people's houses though not of other things like window peeping and arson and vandalism, and there's no telling how long these other things would have gone on, too, but about then I met Carla who had just moved to town from Mississippi and her father was my football coach and that August night when she walked into the grocery store and I was talking to Mason, he said, "I'd like to be the guy who's getting that" and I said, "Me, too," and by God pretty soon I actually was. One night I asked her to go for a ride in my car and we went to park not at the lane with the buried bottles where we would later get stuck but just on the outskirts of town where now there are houses. I stopped the car and pulled her to me and it wasn't like it was with Margaret not letting me stick my tongue in her mouth no, this girl was warm to touch. And I felt under her blouse and between her legs and it was hot like fire down there even outside her shorts, because this first time

I didn't put my hand inside them but only felt the warmth from her skin through the fabric and it was hot, there was heat there, and I never broke into anyone's house again after that, I didn't even think about it, I'd found something new to do, but that is another story.

A Date

I made a date with a girl I met at work. She was a freelance re-searcher and visual artist who had been working at a prestigious design studio but got shit-canned when they decided to cut back on staff. So her self-esteem was pretty low and working doing paste-ups of designs for some moronic football jerseys wasn't rais-ing it any higher.

When I got to her apartment in Queens she was drinking a beer and I thought, "Oh, no, not another alcoholic." I'd hooked up with some heavy drinkers in the past and it never turned out worth a damn. They were always saying they'd call and not doing it or forgetting to show up, and then it was even more annoying to have to listen to their apologies and excuses than it was not to see them in the first place. She finished the beer she was drinking and started another one and I thought to myself, "Oh, well. Might as well try to fuck her tonight and then forget about it."

So we went to the movie we had picked to see. We got there twenty minutes early so she suggested we go to the bar next door. She had another beer there and we were ten minutes late for the beginning of the film, something I hate. "I'm sorry we're late," she said. "I don't care," I said.

I thought the movie was funny but she thought it was bad. She didn't like the popcorn either. That was about the only thing we had agreed on so far. After the movie we went to a falafel joint and she had shish kabob and two more beers. I wasn't drinking at all.

A Date

Walking back to her apartment I put my arm around her waist and kissed her. She let me do it and even tongued back a little. Her breath was a mixture of meat, beer, and tobacco. It tasted good.

We went upstairs to her place and sat on the couch. She was slurring her words. I moved next to her and started licking her ears and neck. The first time I went for her breast she put a hand up to stop me, but five minutes later she didn't. I unbuttoned her blouse and got my fingers inside her bra while I kept working on her neck and ears. Next I undid her belt and started worming my hand down into her underwear. It was hard to get a good angle but I managed to do it without hurting my wrist too much. After about fifteen minutes of these contortions I asked her if she wanted to go to bed and she said yes. I was ripping my shirt off and undoing my pants when she said, "This is going too fast for me." I just kept my hand moving between her legs. By now I was up on the bed beside her and she was humping my arm. Then I was on top of her. I was thrusting and she was thrusting back. We were a pair of thrusters. I came but she didn't, she was too drunk. When we were done she said, "I didn't expect this to happen." "Neither did I," I said, lying. We went to sleep.

The next morning we ate bagels and didn't talk about the night before. She walked me to the subway and we both said we had had a good time and made a date for the next Saturday, which she broke. We haven't spoken since.

Going Home

According to the plumber something is plugging up the works. He's gone off to get some sort of a damn stick with a gadget on the end of it to run down in there. I asked him what happened to his brother. The last time both of them came. He said, "I lost my bud, he had a cancer. My bud, he knew animals. One place we worked their mule was acting funny and my bud said, 'Get some salt meat grease, that mule's hurting.' I came back with a bucket of grease. He took some and ran his hand up the shaft where the mule's dick was. He spread it around in there and in a minute the mule's dick came out. It was two feet long. The shaft had gotten filled up with dirt blowing inside it and he couldn't get his dick out to piss. If you were in that condition you'd act funny, too. When it came out it was covered with big scales of dry caked dirt. It was the awfullest thing you've ever seen."

I sympathized. I told him I lost my mother not too long ago. Her sarcophagus is on order. Copy of an ancient tomb, only two others in existence according to the ad. The Roman noble Scipio's if I'm not mistaken, in granite. His was rifled.

Mother used to visit me here on occasion, but her permanent residence was in a sort of asylum for the aged and the infirm, where her body and I presume her soul clawed on thanks to an annuity I provided, anonymously of course, to spare her pride, and also to avoid in our relations anything that smacked of gratitude.

It is a fact that people will cram themselves down your throat, if you let them, just to show how terrifically grateful they are, until you gag on it and swear to keep to yourself in the future. But I'm satisfied she had no inkling of my little device, and that if she came to see me it was for her own benefit, not mine.

I paid Mother a visit at the home just once, and I never went back. It was a cozy enough place to putrefy in, convenient to the cemetery and the church not far away either. Judging by her rate of disintegration I figured she was good for another decade at the most, barring new discoveries in medicine. Most of the inmates sat benignly in armchairs enjoying any one of several near-comatose states, not always at the public expense. Outside Mother's door an old woman nearly tore the sleeve off my shirt and started shouting, "No no give it to me give it to me I'm thirsty I'm thirsty Joe Joe," and so on, right in my face, everything twice. I don't know who she thought I was.

Mother's roommate turned out to be a congenial old prune named Mrs. Leaf, one hundred and three years old, just one of an impressive number of veritable ancients on the roster. This flabby skeleton had sparkling eyes, no teeth, and was extremely pleasant, smiling and laughing for no reason at all. She obviously knew how to pass the time. For my part I engaged in lighthearted chatter, mostly with myself. For Mother said very little. In fact she said nothing, being preoccupied with the operation of her fluorescent table lamp, a simple affair of a red button and a black button, one on, one off, neither of which she could bring herself to push, though she did execute several promising approaches to both only to retract at the last second. I stayed for lunch. The nurse, an obvious nymphomaniac, wheeled in a cart of trays set with food and brightly colored capsules. She immediately set upon Mrs. Leaf and did her best to spoon a goblet of beige liquid down her throat. Mrs. Leaf wasn't having any. The old battler wasn't going to be browbeaten at this late stage of the game. Over the clatter of falling dishes and Mrs. Leaf's struggling giggles came louder chanting from the hall: "Come here come here the stove the stove Joe Joe Joe Joe Joe . . . . " The shouts grew fainter as the attendants wrestled the troublemaker away. Mrs. Leaf soon passed out with a smile on her face, something they slipped in her water I suspect, and as Mother got terribly interested in the arrangement of the doilies on her bedside table, I took off.

The place fit Mother like a glove. For some time all I had been able to wring out of her were disjointed statements and queries, chiefly of a religious nature. I know where she picked it up, I remember a lot of it myself. She seemed to be stuck on one particular song, a gloomy little tune from some miserable worm-eaten hymnal. The chorus ran "da-di-da fear the grave da-di," just a little something to hum to yourself for consolation at the sad end of a sad day. For no telling how many consecutive years she and I sat through that sort of gloomy trash every Sunday, and I got my belly full of it. But it's funny how I remember those mute hours now with a twinge of bliss. And that only goes to prove that practically anything dredged up from childhood, no matter how repulsive to the present day, knows how to array itself in dulcet hues. The hours I spent in the warm atmosphere of the sanctuary, the sun filtering through windows of ocher and squash, still innocent, still ignorant! I sat at Mother's side, my eyes piously raised to a stained-glass representation of the hills, in this version curiously bare and stony except for a line of firs on the spine of the slopes, which my heretical imagination transformed into two stegosauri, hopeless Biblical impossibilities of course. But the hilly vista did not fail to provide the guaranteed help, as through its intercession I rode out the most seductive temptations, on the one hand to fall asleep, on the other to feast my eyes on the sumptuous figure of Mrs. Burcham in the choir loft, which no robe on earth could disguise. Of course when the choir rose for the Doxology it was all over with me. The Lord Himself would have faltered in the face of that heaving bosom as Mrs. Burcham conquered the upper reaches of the scale. Incidentally I wasn't the only person so skewered. The deacon directly in front of us was shameless in his attentions to the soprano chair. And one obese elder in the rear regularly snored through the entire service, roused only by the benediction. His was a sonorous drone, with now and then a violent snort that woke whole rows from their daydreams. And sometimes, in contrast, his nose whistled like a tea kettle, when a hair or booger got stuck in there sideways for minutes on end. And periodically his great bulk was the epicenter of a series of loud explosions, the product of unpleasant memories or troubled digestion. If the interval between snores seemed too great I began to think he might be dead, and I waited anxiously for the next breath to save him. It came, and I was free again to admire the little girl in a white sundress one pew over, or gaze at the light fixture in the ceiling whose pane was black with bugs roasted to death on the bulb.

It sounds like a frolic, but I knew I was under constant scrutiny. The slightest faux pas and I would be imprisoned in my room for the afternoon. But in later years, during Mother's senescence, it was I who became the custodian. In pity I let her think she was in charge of the kitchen, a grave error as it turned out because she insisted on cooking for me. Her initial coddled eggs were a pitiful runny mess. The simplest things are the first to go I suppose. When I complained she nimbly reversed her field and boiled the eggs over a flame that would have served to char a steer, so that the yolks were overdone and tasted like chalk. Naturally she botched the coffee, too, so that I wound up swilling down this time a thin brown fluid, and the next time having to suck hard to get down a black sludge the consistency of porridge. And speaking of porridge, the mess she made of the oatmeal makes me want to puke just thinking about it. Oh, she made a big deal out of it, flourishing the pot and spoon and stirring and singing, just like she knew what was going on, but the results I found in my bowl spoke volumes of her talents, being either a sticky paste or a number of lumpy clods. And the way Mother herself ate, always drooling, I don't want to think about it, it made me sick.

Yet this same pathetic being in her better days had charge of me, her duty as she saw it to curb the excesses of my youth. One memorable spring I was in love, delirious and intoxicated beyond all reason, in hot pursuit of Marie, a girl from Sunday School. I was enflamed, the weather was balmy, and I spent a giddy Sunday afternoon of a church outing chasing after her, making a fool of myself. When the group went fishing I pointed out the best fishing spots in a loud voice, like an impresario, or someone of importance at any rate, then stood by triumphantly as fish after hapless fish was barbarously hooked and jerked out of the water, left to flap and suffocate in the choking weeds. It worked. I caught Marie's eye and won her over. At dusk we sat side by side around the fire and sang devotional songs. The group was loud and cheerful, in a word far too much like a Sunday School outing, from which it is almost impossible to escape without notice. We ate weenies. The conversations went on, I have no doubt on the most trivial topics imaginable. Horses were mentioned. Marie said she adored them, so I seized on the pretext to lead her to the stables. As we walked across a long, dark lawn I put my arm around her waist. She reciprocated. This was encouraging, in fact I couldn't have done without it. In no time we were in the stables and going at it like professionals on a horse blanket. She had all the right parts, as near as I could make out, and perfect teeth. There wasn't much to it, a few grunts from her and some ill-conceived thrashing on my part. The mosquitoes were exceedingly fierce. A horse had its head over the stall watching us. She reached up and rubbed its face, something I never do, due to some terrifying experiences as a child.

Well, Mother got wind of this little escapade. One of her lieutenants must have blabbed on us. She didn't get all the facts though, judging by the nature of her accusations. Or maybe she was too embarrassed to refer to the more repugnant details. She confined herself to the declaration of the following law, namely that she wouldn't have me running with sluts, risking infection and disease. And in this connection she brought up the edifying but seldom mentioned case of my syphilitic Uncle Bunn, an agronomist of some note who brought down great suffering upon him and his, a judgment, Mother said, on his reckless youth. In spite of his disease Bunn married and begat a child upon his wife. The child wasn't right. It was off-center. It died young and that was considered a good thing. Later Bunn himself went up the flume. In his dying delirium his agricultural visions were magnificent. He began sanely enough, with a reasoned discourse insisting that the idea that the Hessian fly attacks oats has absolutely no foundation in nature. And he plowed a fairly straight furrow with the sobering information that St. John's weed has the peculiarity of affecting only white-haired animals, though it will act just as lethally upon a red-haired animal with white hair around its nose or feet. But he began to lose his grip on the subject of the guinea pig, which he said could be eaten, though generally speaking they are not disposed of in this manner, and finally he signaled his approaching end by an aroused and obscene monologue on the properties of boar semen, a gelatinous material resembling tapioca.

To put an end to my lascivious ways I was sent to work for Mr. Tate, a dyspeptic storekeeper, in accordance with the theory, not altogether without merit, that hard work would keep me from mischief. And I did a pretty good job right up until I was fired for a bit of mayhem involving his prize sow. In front of the store was a muddy depression in great favor with this enormous female. She generally lay there from morning to dusk, when the sirenic calls of Mr. Tate lured her to the trough several blocks away. At the first sound of his whooping she would struggle from the wallow to her feet and with rapid little steps make her way home, a pilgrimage graven in the twilight since prehistoric times it seemed. This sow, Zella by name, was the esteemed mother of scores, including on one notable occasion (to the astonishment of Mr. Tate, who left the whelping room in disbelief only to return after a shot of whiskey to verify what he had seen) a two-headed piglet that was sadly short-lived. One morning, before Zella showed up to man her station, I took it into my head to pour three quarts of turpentine into her puddle. Zella arrived, rooted about distractedly, and with the naive trust of the domestic animal settled happily down into a perfect hell. Within seconds she began to grunt uncomfortably, then abruptly rose and ran off, with considerable interest, in search of relief. This galloping in itself was a serious matter, as Mr. Tate wouldn't appreciate the fat she was running off, nor the hazard to her limbs as she careened down the street. Yet more serious was the calamity of portly Mrs. Nelson, out for her morning constitutional, who was trampled flat when the tormented pig ran between her legs. Along with incalculable damage to her dignity she suffered a hairline fracture of the wrist. So in a sense my dismissal was purely medicinal, a forfeit to salve the spiritual and physical wounds endured by Mrs. Nelson, who not coincidentally was a heavy consumer of the various female compounds sold at the store.

Uncle Bunn mad, Mother mad, it's a regular epidemic. Most of the time she didn't anymore know where she was than shit on a stick. Oh, I don't doubt that occasionally some feeble light made its way upward from the bottom of the mess, taking the form perhaps of a little mental picture, or maybe just a feeling, vague dread for instance, that lasted the length of a shudder then vanished, another speck in the dust bin. She began to resurrect the dead, including her cat, whom I am convinced by the way was an atheist, and station them on the sofa. It didn't bother me, I was used to it, but it did tend to shake up the guests when she referred to them as her deceased mother or father, or as both, turn and turn again. And if by a stroke of luck she got the person's name right, and even hit a streak where her first two or three statements made a little sense, by her fourth or fifth utterance something was bound to escape her lips that struck an anxious chord in the visitor's stomach, and by the sixth or seventh she was rattling off things so utterly mad that she had the thoroughly spooked guest smiling and nodding in assent while frantically casting about the room for his wrap, which I had cunningly lodged in an inaccessible closet at the back of the house. But they never had to squirm for long, because Mother would suddenly jump up and leave the room without so much as a comma, thinking she was being paged in a railroad station or being wheeled away to the delivery room to have a baby.

That she confused the living and the dead was no big deal, often the difference is so slight as to make this a very sound point of view. And her custom of wiping her rear end with the cotton bath towels wasn't an insuperable problem; I simply kept mine under lock and key and destroyed hers every month or so. But when her wits scattered like chaff, when objects, those boundary stones for the world of accredited reality, lost for her all intelligibility, so that she wore her panties on her head for a hat, mistook her bureau for the stove and reduced it to ashes, and dipped drinking water from the toilet bowl when she was thirsty, delights foresworn by the tiniest infant imbecile, given the proper training of course, well, it got to be an aggravation.

One day the home called. Your mother is loose, they said. She's bound to show up there by dark, they added. We'll be by to round her up. Fine, I said, all three times. I told my man Del to stand watch at the gate. He threw a fit. Said he'd quit and get a job with the railroad. I didn't blame him, I'd just about had it with those jackasses myself. If they couldn't hold back a skinny demented old woman, though admittedly fiercely determined and far from frail, what good were they at all? They were lucky to get her in the first place. All things considered she had had an ideal situation with her room above the café in town. A fat woman ran the place, keeping her father, my mother, and thirty cats upstairs. It's not imaginable, but I think Mother and the old man had some sort of a romance going on. The fires are not quenched even near the end it would seem. Anyway, Mother did the cooking (good God!), the fat woman guarded the door with a mesh flyswatter, and her father tended counter. This old man had too much blood. The doctors had to siphon a pint a week out of him. In my opinion his condition was caused at least in part by his overweening hatred of mailmen, who he said always tore his magazines to shreds, after reading them at the post office for a week or two, of course. He paid taxes, their salaries in fact, supported their families, by God he practically owned the goddamned post office, and the treatment he got from those impudent piss-ants in return was a disgrace. But in general all was well in this little household. Then the fat woman and her boyfriend decamped, or eloped, at any rate left her father and Mother in the lurch. The shock shoved the old man over the brink. While I packed Mother's things he chattered a tale how on a porch in India he had grabbed a hoe and chopped snakes for half an hour. Then he moved on to Australia where he and four service buddies were locked overnight in a Pullman with six whores. We left him riding machete in hand into a panicked village in the jungles of South America, where smack dab in the middle of the marketplace a boa constrictor was swallowing the town goat, and no one lifting a finger to save it.

Anyway, I smoothed things over with Del. He just had the piles that day. He threatens to quit every time a frog pisses. He took up his post at the gate and I went inside to clean my pistol. It was impossible to predict these visits of Mother's. In order to reach me she first had to get clear of the home, a flight made all the more difficult since much of the time she was restrained, as they put it, by straps. I never learned what subterfuge delivered her from the grounds, much less by what means she was able to locomote cross-country. She would surge out of the blue toting a box of chocolates, the very one, I am confident, sent by me each week to the home. "I'm on furlough," she would say. I didn't dispute that statement, nor did I dispute anything else she might hazard to declare. She would take a seat and proceed to flounder in and out of a number of moods of extraordinary variety, several of which I was on the verge of pinning down with some accuracy here in the wild, so to speak. For instance, sometimes she must have thought she was young again. She would flirt with some invisible suitor, batting her ruined eyelashes, tossing her last three strands of hair as though she had a flowing mane. In brief, the best approximation of a coquette she could muster, given her resources, a frightful display. Then when the attendants from the home materialized to retrieve her, she called them hyenas and other gross epithets, abusing them in a foul and shocking manner until the injection took effect and her limp form slid from view inside the maw of the ambulance.

Mother's previous visit had been most illuminating. She let me in on the news that she had recently visited heaven, where she spoke with God and all of her kinfolk, including mercifully her own poor mother, who was bitten in the bloom of life by a hydrophobic rat terrier and suffered the usual horrible death consequent. This circumstance turned Mother against dogs to the extent that she made a cat her closest companion. Kitty was a mean but charming little pet she rescued from certain death at the hands of a pack of snarling dogs bent on having her for supper. Mother waded into them with a broom handle and emerged holding a naked furless scrap of a kitten. This trauma so early in her career no doubt accounts for

Kitty's suspicious nature, and hence her long life. Just to persuade her to eat you had to stand at the top of the steps and shout "Here Kitty Kitty Kitty Kitty Kitty!" until your lungs burst, and only then would she peek from under a bush three feet away and warily come forward for her meal. I believe Kitty was determined to die a natural death, unattended by the fury of blood and crushing of bones so woefully common in the annals of her race. And sure enough in the end she was undone not by her enemy the dog but by some internal disorder that was rotting her insides. She mewled hideously for days before the veterinarian could crawl under the house and dispatch her, whether with a pill or a ball bat I really don't know.

I waited all that afternoon, a bit anxious, all sorts of thoughts running through my head. But Mother didn't show up. I was about to pack it in when three gentlemen from the home talked their way past Del, there's nothing easier, and came into the house. It took me a while to understand what they were getting at. "Your mother is dead" was the gist of their message. It seems Mother had refused to eat for several days. Then she disappeared. They found her collapsed in a cornfield. In that case maybe she wasn't on her way to see me at all, but merely gone out to graze. At least they found her before the crows got to her. That could have been a real mess. The gentlemen were embarrassed about the matter, understandably so. They wouldn't leave, just sat around hemming and hawing for the better part of an hour. I listened to all of their apologies and excuses then fired three shots into the wall over their heads. Then they couldn't get out the door fast enough. I got a hat out of the affair. I doubt they'll return for it.

There was a funeral. Mother looked like a sturgeon, in spite of the embalmer's best efforts. But it didn't matter, she was out of mortal hands long before, long before. I like to fancy she has a place in the celestial choir, perhaps singing alongside Mrs. Burcham, who burst a vein in mid-cantata one Easter, singing of release and light and the souls yet caught in sin's dark dungeon. To tell the truth Mother wasn't much of a singer on earth, but who knows what gifts are given above, where she basks now, in recompense for toil below, where still I think she slogs across a dreary plain, plying toward me.

Unction

I was in Veronica's apartment, waiting for her and her new boyfriend to come back, rustling through her lingerie drawer looking for her brassieres. I found one from Saks Fifth Avenue and five or six from Macy's, most of them simple white cotton but two of them black lacy ones that I had bought her. There were other clothes, too: her French sailor jersey with blue and white stripes, her sweaters, including the dark blue one she wore the last time I saw her, a white one she wore with her tight red skirt, and the light gray cashmere I gave her with the v-neck that showed off her cleavage. I saw the nightgown I bought her for her birthday and my favorite skirt, the black and white dotted silk one her friend Martha made for her that yielded so easily to the touch when she lay back on the bed, so easily swept aside to reveal the high cut of her hips and her tan lines.

It was early, just nine o'clock. It was a pretty good bet that she and Roger wouldn't return for a couple of more hours, so I went into one of her roommates' rooms and looked around. There wasn't much to see there—I wasn't interested in Audrey's clothes and she kept her room so spartan that nothing seemed sexy about it at all. I went back into the living room and looked in Veronica's desk for letters she might have gotten from Kent, the boyfriend she had lived with before I met her, the one she always threw up to me as the man she had really been in love with. The whole time we'd gone out I'd never even looked at a photo of him. I hadn't wanted to know what he looked like. They'd lived together in Greece in a house on the beach and she'd always told me that the two of them were going to have been married, but after a couple of months of hearing from her about how fabulous this guy was I finally asked her if she and Kent had actually talked about getting married and she said no, they hadn't, and then I began to suspect the entire story, which according to her went like this: They were in love. They were perfectly suited for each other. They loved to travel together. They went to Africa, where Kent got mad at her because she wasn't adapting well to the environment (I never found out what that meant). They returned to Greece. She went to Spain for a month to help her younger brother open a new business, telling Kent before she left that if there were any problems in their relationship not to tell her because she was going to be so busy she wouldn't have time to deal with it. Then while she was in Spain she slept with a golf pro. I asked her why she slept with the golf pro, since she and Kent had agreed to be monogamous, and at first she said she'd done it because she could tell things weren't going well, but then she admitted she might have slept with the golf pro regardless of how things were going.

So now I was ready to look at this guy's photo and I saw a sort of medium good-looking man who seemed like he might drink a little too much and wouldn't take kindly to his girlfriend sleeping with a golf pro in Spain. I guess that's why when she came back Kent told her it was all over. He wouldn't sleep with her, he would hardly talk to her. She stayed two weeks begging him to reconsider and he was cold as ice. Finally she left and fucked somebody in Italy and someone else in France and then came home to the family she was trying to escape. There were lots of pictures of them: her father whom she fought with every time she went home; her mother who was always on and off different weight-loss schemes that were inevitably undermined by food binges; her older brother who seemed to have escaped unscathed and was married and raising a family in California. Her father had liked me. "You're the only boyfriend I've had that he would talk to," she said. Her father even took her aside and told her, "You want to know how he rates? He's the best boyfriend you've ever had." I felt flattered because chronologically according to her I was number fifty-something on the list (Veronica said she was always surprised when she saw her cervix in the gynecologist's mirror at how pink and fresh she looked inside). But it was small consolation now because in the end she had said she wasn't happy and needed to move on and we split up and she wound up meeting Roger in a bookstore and going with him the same day back to his apartment and now she was seeing him instead of me and now he was number fifty-something plus one.

At about nine-thirty I thought about turning on the TV, but I had an urge to masturbate so I went into Veronica's bedroom and put on one of her brassieres and a pair of her panties and kneeled in front of the mirror by the African wood statuette and jerked off. It wasn't anything too elaborate, I just felt the soft skirt and occasionally sniffed it and smelled the sweater where her perfume lingered, the perfume she always wore, Roree, which I had gotten for her at Christmas. She had kept saying "I can't believe you got me this!" because I'd sprung for the one hundred and fifty dollar bottle. The masturbation was satisfactory, it seemed dangerous enough and I came on a pair of her panties and put them back in the drawer. Then I lay back on the bed and thought about Roger and her. I couldn't figure out why she was with him. He talked so much he could make the simplest conversation an ordeal. The only thing I could figure was that she wanted someone she wasn't going to fall in love with. He had a car so they could go to the beach, and since he was somebody I knew, she also knew I would find out about it pretty quickly, and that was a big plus. Because even though she was the one who instigated all of our breakups (by my count there had been at least four major ones) she always got furious and upset and jealous each time when she found out I was seeing someone else and did everything she could to wreck my new relationship. It didn't take much, usually a drunken phone call where she sobbed and cried and begged me to see her. "She wants to keep you in a little box," my Argentine friend Maria told me. "She's a loser," my American friend Barbara told me. "Stay away from her," all my other friends told me and I tried, but she knew she could call me up and cry and say she had to see me and I'd meet her at Water's Edge or at Fanelli's or at Risolio's and we would drink and make out and go home and fuck our brains out and I would take her back, at least until the last time when she didn't come back, she started fucking Roger instead, and that was that.

After a while I went into her other roommate's room to look in her diary for any mentions of me and Veronica, but there weren't any. Patricia was a lesbian most of the time, though a year before she'd dated a man for a while. She didn't know what to do with him in bed. "What do you do with the dick?" she asked Veronica. I left her room, went into the kitchen, and drank a glass of cranberry juice. I noticed that there was still a photograph of me on the refrigerator. It didn't have to mean anything, because the whole side of the refrigerator was covered with various photos, magnets, drawings her nieces had made and grocery lists. But it was there. I went back into the living room and turned the television on to a televangelist: "If you don't follow instructions, God will administer the rod of correction. If you don't get the lesson right, God will administer the rod of correction. It's like putting a pure soul in the garbage can. If you don't have unction in your heart he'll leave you in that mess. You'll sit in the stink. You'll live in the stink. You'll breathe the stink. Until finally you say out loud, 'Get me out of here. I'll never do it again!' God can feed you in a dry and thirsty land. You wonder how you're living? You're living because God is putting manna down! Hunh! Hunh! Hunh!" I turned the TV off and sat down on the couch.

I thought back to the day at the beach, Montauk, three months before, when we had broken up for the final time. We had a horrible time that day. We fought about everything, about the sandwiches, the sunscreen, the beach umbrella. We tried to calm down by taking a walk on the beach. We saw a couple fucking in the dunes, then we ran into a gay friend of Veronica's who couldn't take his eyes off her breasts (she'd taken her top off). "I don't think I'll ever be able to look at you in quite the same way," he said. On the train on the way home we hardly spoke, except when Veronica told me about her trip to Antigua where an eighty-year-old man sitting by the ocean asked her for a cigarette then asked if she would fuck him, communicating by making the universal sign of the index finger sliding in and out of his loosely clenched fist. We didn't spend the night together and then a week later we broke up in a restaurant in Little Italy.

All these memories got me turned on so I went back to Veronica's room and started jerking off again. Beneath me I felt the soft sheets where we had lain making love for three hours at a time. I remembered her lying there saying "That was the best, that was it, that was so good" over and over again with my come still inside her and her tan belly and tan breasts heaving gently past the point of spasm and her wet hair sticking to her forehead with my fingers pressed lightly against her temple and the smell of sex in the air and in the sheets. I came on my stomach this time and rolled over and rubbed the come into the sheets where she and Roger would be lying soon. It was almost ten o'clock and Veronica didn't usually stay out much beyond eleven on a Sunday night. There wasn't much time left.

I found my pants and pulled out two notes I'd written. The

first said: "You are the lowest piece of shit human being I've ever met. I hate your fucking guts. Fuck off." The second said, "I miss you. I love you. Call me." I put them both back into my pocket. At about ten-thirty I went into the bathroom. I opened the medicine cabinet, took the bottle of Roree perfume out and poured the contents down the drain. It wasn't even the bottle I'd bought her, because the last time I saw her—six weeks ago on a Monday night she had shown up at my house drunk, spent the night, and we had fucked in the morning—I smelled it on her and mentioned it and she said she and her roommates had used up what I got her and now were on a new bottle. But I figured it belonged to me, if only by proxy. So I poured it down the drain and then I stole a pair of her white cotton underwear and one of her white cotton brassieres, and stuffed them in my pocket, and I broke a leg off the African wood statuette because she had gotten it when she was with Kent who she had said she was still in love with all the time she was with me, and I saw the come still wet on the bed and I was ready to go. I was guilty of breaking and entering, or just entering, since all I had done was climb up the fire escape in the back because she always left her window unlocked, and criminal mischief perhaps because after all I did crack the statue's leg and waste the perfume. I regretted that a little, it would have been better just to leave the wet spot on the bed and in her panties, but my emotions got the better of me. At eleven o'clock I climbed back out the fire escape, went down into the yard, and left by the building three doors down. I could have waited outside until she and Roger came home and watched her slide down drunkenly on the bed and take Roger's hand and pull him to her to make love on the wet spot that they wouldn't notice because they would be too drunk and too involved in making another wet spot they would fall asleep on, but it was chilly, I was spent and now I just wanted to get on the subway and go home. On the *R* train I imagined her finding the empty perfume bottle in the morning and being puzzled, and maybe later in the day noticing the statuette's broken leg, and who knew what she would think? What did it really matter anyway? I was the one who had no unction in my heart. I was the one living in the stink. I was the one who wanted to scream, "Lord, get me out of here. I'll never do it again!"

Legacy

On the last day of April
the most venereal of months
in the forty-first year of life
having had—to date—a single surgical intervention
this being the insertion of an apparatus like a garden hose
down the throat of my pecker
with cutting attachments to remove
a so-called stricture of the urethra
so that the flow of urine might be more free,
I hereby declare my desire to die and my
imminent leave-taking of life.

That being of disturbed mind and diseased testicles
I, John of Mung, do hereby make the following bequests
after the will of God
to the extent it is known to me
and requesting forgiveness for all my ignorances
and transgressions
Domine Domine etcetera:

To the Italian doctor
who undertook this most unnecessary
and ill-conceived operation
I leave the prick of a dead rooster and the nuts of a rutting boar

both to be placed inside his living mouth
and there sewn up with fishing line through his lying lips
meaning no harm to his reputation
which is excellent
or to his standing among his colleagues
who read his papers in the medical journals.

To the Irish anesthesiologist
who provided the blessed sodium pentothal
and offered a smiling Irish face floating above my flimsy gown
and shaved pubis
I leave the memory of all my loves past
which list is now complete and final
from the first in a silk nightgown
in the attic of her parents' house
to the last a blow job in a parking lot outside a nightclub
from a drunken barmaid infected with God knows what ailments
all loves shared and requited and unrequited
I leave these memories to that Irish angel of anesthesia.

To the Jamaican nurse
who brought the great drug Percoset
to dull my senses and take my mind off the bloody piss
flowing into the clear plastic satchel at the end of my catheter
I leave the extensive library of my writings both poetry and prose
that fills four drawers of a filing cabinet
and yet which for all that has brought me
in my fifteen years of professional life
the grand sum of five thousand three hundred
and forty-eight dollars
the bulk of that in one grant from the state,
to her I leave in that filing cabinet my soul bared in writing
worth less than the price of a cheap used car.

Legacy

To my German hospital roommate
age eighty-four
who underwent a transabdominal prostatectomy
and who bled gouts of blood into his satchel
and nearly died of clots in his bladder
I leave my previous desire to have a long life, to be a sage
I have seen the sages
they are all in the hospital having dick operations
to my roommate in thanks for the revelation that old age
is nothing but disease and pain and suffering of indignities
and medical abuse, I leave my desire to be old.

To my Hindu urologist
who now monthly probes my rectum with his Vedic forefinger
and finds bogginess and inflammation and prostatic disturbance
I leave the philosophy and religion both east and west
that have brought me to such a pass that my dick will not answer
to any god but the god of pain,
and all this I now embrace and discard so at the moment of death
God grant that it be swift
I will find what is needed to guide me safely
into the realms of the afterworld.

To my friends and acquaintances of all nationalities
I leave my belongings
the shoes I have saved
the coats shirts socks clocks
the accumulated trash of thirty-eight years
let them be burned or saved or sold or given away
and let each reclaim that of theirs
which I have borrowed stolen or appropriated as my own
(they will know by sight what these things are)
and let them forgive and remember
and pray for the further journeys of this soul.

The Sexual Life of Savages

Enough enough time's up no more mewling get on with it
let us dull the senses with Percoset with alcohol with oven gas
in memory of all those suicides
the fraternity of souls doomed to the world of hell
welcome all those spirits
let the bells ring the torches flare the feast begin
a feast in hell to welcome the new arrivals
a festival a new beginning
the true source of all pleasure is death
I embrace it without witnesses
only my name affixed in surety to this document
the last day of the venereal month of April
the light is fading
good good I go
misericordia misericordia etcetera.

—JOHN OF MUNG

Dinner

So I was sitting in a restaurant with this woman I had a severe crush on and all I could do was tell her how badly all my past love affairs had turned out. I must have been really nervous. I'd never been to that restaurant before, I had worked late and barely made it there on time, and then once we got seated and began our conversation the maître d' came over and said he had made an error and would we mind moving to another table. Still, I don't think it was any of that stuff that threw me but more the fact that the woman, her name is Anna, is married and has a two-year-old daughter and I was just experiencing all the guilt I would feel if I told her I had a crush on her and she said she felt the same way and we had an affair and it wound up destroying her marriage and her family. So instead I started talking about this young girl at work who I also had a crush on, a blond twenty-four-year-old whose only flaws were dandruff and a recurring staph infection on her forehead that made a huge red welt appear there every couple of months or so, but who was really quite beautiful and just strange enough to be intriguing and not annoying.

Anna was telling me I should pursue this girl and sleep with her and I was coming up with all these reasons why not, that the girl had a boyfriend, that she was only twenty-four, that it would be awkward to work with someone I was involved with, that it would be even more awkward to work with someone I had told I had a crush on if she didn't feel the same way, that it would be disastrous to work with someone I had had an affair with that turned out badly. Anna wasn't believing any of this, she just said go ahead and ask the girl out, do it on Monday (this was Friday night). I was getting even more confused because Anna seemed to be flirting with me, and I knew I was flirting with her, and there we were having a kind of love affair by proxy through discussing the girl at work with the staph infection.

Dinner came and mine wasn't too good, the chicken wasn't cooked as well as I like it and the spinach tasted funny. Anna was eating sea bass and drinking her second glass of wine. She'd had a long day casting actors for a movie she was involved with, and since she had come in from California she was having trouble going to sleep at night. She had gotten a joint from someone the night before and tried to smoke it, but it was so small, every time she tried to light it the flame from the match scorched the end of her nose, until finally the joint was all burned up and she didn't even get a hit off it. She hoped the wine would do the trick. She seemed to be getting a little drunk and I started thinking maybe I should get drunk, too, and then maybe something would happen. I remembered a few times when alcohol greased the wheels of desire to the point where a situation like this turned into a romantic evening. But I couldn't drink alcohol because I had an amoeba in my intestines that had been wreaking havoc for the previous six months and I was taking anti-flagellants and herbal treatments to kill off the little unicellular bastard. Since alcohol taken with my medications could lead to nausea and vomiting, I just drank water.

As I was going on about my love affairs I mentioned the fact that a number of them had been with married women, that somehow I find it safer even though it can be a little anxiety provoking at moments, like the time a lover's husband pulled out his shotgun and threatened to splatter first her and then himself all over the dining room ceiling unless she told him who she was sneaking around with. Anna asked me why I got involved with married women and I went into the whole long tale of my emotional history as it has been revealed to me in analysis, all that stuff about my father and mother and family that has somehow conspired to make an emotional idiot out of me, and I'm thinking, "This is all wrong, this isn't what I should be saying, I should be telling her I'm crazy about her, use the honesty approach, it worked last fall with that actress and we wound up going to her apartment and fucking on her living room floor."

But then I think about the fact that this is really the first time I've been alone with Anna even though I've known her for years, because before she was always with her boyfriend or her husband, and it seems presumptuous and inappropriate to just burst out gushing how much I like her, an embarrassment that would ruin not only this evening but any chance of future developments. Still, I know she was interested in seeing me because she told our friend Cynthia to tell me she was coming to town and Cynthia had made a point of instructing me to call her because Anna would be too shy to call me. But instead of saying anything I just sit there daydreaming about how any minute now Anna is going to invite me back to her hotel, which for this visit is the old Arden Hotel up on Seventy-Fourth Street, which has seen better days and is remarkable for its dearth of hot water and the way the wind whistles through the windows at night while you're trying to sleep.

And then Anna starts telling me how she met her husband, how she moved to L.A. and he lived in the house next door, she was dating another guy and when that didn't work out she started seeing Robert, and I'm thinking that's the first time she has mentioned Robert all night which is a good sign. Another good sign comes almost immediately afterward when she starts telling how she wants to take a trip across the country, just her and her daughter (she's not getting along very well with Robert just now, and she's feuding with his family), and as she is talking I start having a fantasy that it's me riding in the car with her instead of the little girl, and we drive down all the old highways visiting Civil War battlefields and National Parks, stopping for the night in Gallup, New Mexico, where all the motels are run by Indians from India and the streets are filled with Indians from North America, or maybe we pull into the Alamo Motel in Memphis where I used to work and was held up by two men wielding ax-handles. Then I hear her saying the point of the trip is to visit Barry Shelton in Virginia and I wonder if that means she is having an affair with him, or if she just travels across the country collecting admirers who have crushes on her and that enables her to stay in her marriage without jeopardizing it by going so far as to have actual affairs. This is all very confusing to me and I haven't had a single sip of alcohol, while she is on her third glass of wine and slurring her words a little and I am telling her how I've always been attracted to brunettes (she's a brunette), probably because when I was a baby I had a black nanny whose name was Faith Hope Charity Smith, after the Bible verse in Corinthians, who was called Charity by everybody, because the verse says "the greatest of these is charity."

Then we're getting the check, she's paying because she's on an expense account, and we get up and I'm the one who feels drunk. It's pleasant out, the rain has stopped and the air is warm for February, and we walk through the streets of SoHo talking about how much it has changed in fifteen years, bodegas into boîtes, storefronts into restaurants and galleries that all seem so glittery and lifeless, an observation that probably isn't even true, we're just expressing our preference for dilapidation. We move into the Village, past Bleecker Street, and Anna says she had vowed to herself not to come to this part of town, it's where she lived with her former boyfriend Steven for six years and that relationship had ended badly, she had moved away, left him to move to California and they had ping-ponged back and forth across the country until she broke it off, she doesn't say what it was that caused her to leave, but it still pains her, even more since she called Steven two weeks ago to tell him she was coming to town and he told her he didn't want to talk to her. For how long, she had said, six months? A year? Two years? Ten years? All he would say was, "I don't want to talk to you."

We passed along Fourth Street, where we saw people dancing in a restaurant and stopped to watch. Anna said she danced at home but never in public, and I told her about the Christmas party at work, where people drank furiously from noon into the night and danced like maniacs in the hotel ballroom and kept drinking until they were sick, then went to a club where one of the men was planting hickies all over his secretary's neck and upper bosom in plain view of his staff who knew he was married and had three kids, and where one of the female designers got punched in the face by a tough New Jersey girl who objected to being jostled on the dance floor.

At last we're on the final block before my apartment and Anna is telling me how she wrote me a long letter four months ago after she read a story I sent her, saying how deeply it affected her, but the letter was too sentimental and she never sent it. I tell her to send it anyway, I want to know what these sentiments are that she is ashamed of, maybe they are the same ones I'm having. It seems like something is just on the verge of happening, that the moment has come when all those feelings will have to come bursting out, that she will say something or I will say something and we'll tell the cab we've just flagged to go on, we've changed our minds, or we'll both get in and ride to the Arden Hotel, getting started in the backseat, not caring what the driver sees. But she doesn't say it and I don't say it and she gets inside alone, and through the open window I say, "When are you coming back," and she says, "Three months." "Call me," I say, "I will," she says. "Send me a postcard," she says, "I will," I say, and that's it, I close the cab door and she and it speed away up First Avenue, out of the East Village, out of New York, out of the East, across Tennessee and Texas, back through New Mexico and Arizona, back to Southern California, the Golden State, back to her husband, back to her child, back to her husband's family she is feuding with, all the way back.

Achieving Equanimity

Now after so many months of torment I'm finally starting to get some distance on this thing, to feel more like myself and not

FUCK YOU YOU CUNT YOU LOUSY BITCH I HATE YOUR FUCKING GUTS

be so prey to the jealous thoughts and anger against her that have kept me up many nights and awakened me from sleep since

AND FUCK THAT ASSHOLE AL HE'S A LOSER JUST LIKE YOU HE'S THE

our parting of the ways. I've come to realize that the relationship which seemed to promise me everything might not

MOST BORING PIECE OF SHIT YOU COULD HAVE PICKED UP CAN'T YOU

have been the best thing for me. There were a lot of problems that never got resolved, which were masked by our

DO ANY BETTER THAN THAT? AT LEAST I DIDN'T GET ANY INCURABLE

attempts to try to find a way for us to express the feelings we had for each other in a way we both could respect and still get

DISEASES GOOD GOD HOW MANY TIMES DID WE HAVE TO TAKE

what we needed. The pain that I've been feeling I've come to realize is not derived solely from this loss but comes from

ANTIBIOTICS YOU'RE A WALKING PETRI DISH I SHOULD SOAK MY DICK IN

other, deeper losses that hearken back to childhood, and to try
to find the solace for that is putting too much of a burden on

FORMALDEHYDE BEFORE I USE IT AGAIN IF I SEE THE TWO OF YOU

another person. We each did the best we could, and even if that
wasn't good enough, and certain actions of hers caused me

TOGETHER ON THE STREET YOU'LL BE LUCKY IF I DON'T SPIT IN YOUR

grief, it does me no good to harbor anger in my heart. That's a
destructive way of dealing with emotions. Compassion and

FUCKING FACES. WHAT A KICK IN THE BALLS ONE WEEK YOU'RE SAYING

forgiveness, though hard to obtain, bring the only relief in
a situation like this. I've increased my daily practice to

HOW MUCH YOU LOVE ME THE NEXT YOU'RE JERKING THIS GUY OFF IN

one hour and a quarter, forty-five minutes in the morning and
half an hour in the evening. I've been reading the lamrim texts on

A HOTEL ROOM AND YOU HAD THE GALL TO TRY TO MITIGATE IT BY

desirous attachment. Desirous attachment is like oil that has
soaked into fabric, while other delusions are like dust that has

SAYING AT LEAST YOU DIDN'T FUCK HIM THAT NIGHT BECAUSE YOU

only settled on its surface. This attachment is difficult to remove
because it has been absorbed into its object so deeply. The texts

HAD A YEAST INFECTION AND IT WASN'T UNTIL TWO WEEKS LATER YOU

also have a lot to say about anger: anger is like a fire that
consumes the merit accumulated from virtuous actions. There is

WERE ABLE TO CONSUMMATE THE AFFAIR ARE YOU FUCKING INSANE?

no evil greater than anger. It harms the person who experiences
it and it harms the people it is directed against. I'm making

YOU THINK IT'S SUPPOSED TO MAKE ME FEEL BETTER THAT YOU ONLY

progress pondering these thoughts and meditating and I can
now begin to have glimpses of a time when my mind will be at

BLEW HIM AND DIDN'T TAKE HIS DICK IN YOUR CUNT THE FIRST

peace with itself and with her, and I'll be able to wish her the
best in her life. Health and happiness. I can even imagine

NIGHT OH GIVE ME A FUCKING BREAK YOU'RE THE BIGGEST

meeting her and her future husband with their child and patting
the little tyke on the head and coming away with a glowing

ASSHOLE I'VE EVER KNOWN I DON'T WANT TO KNOW YOU MY

feeling of the love that I felt before, and having that be a good
feeling. I'm sure it's still a ways off, but I can already feel it

FRIENDS DON'T WANT TO KNOW YOU MY FAMILY HATES YOUR GUTS

growing in me every day. I'm thankful for my studies, for the
growing peace and tranquility I am experiencing and most of

SO JUST FUCK OFF STAY OUT OF MY WAY IF YOU DON'T WANT

all for the opportunity this has given me to learn, grow,
love, and know myself better. May I never be separated

The Sexual Life of Savages

A KICK IN THE CROTCH LIKE THE ONE YOU GAVE ME

for even a minute from the stainless path

YOU ARE THE LOWEST FORM OF LIFE

praised by the Buddhas

GO TO HELL

I Wish I Was Dead

I wish I was dead. I wish I was dead.

My Education

My barber, Ames, came yesterday. Monday is his day off but he drives out here to cut my hair and to get away from his wife. He has to have his Monday bottle. He'd drink hair tonic if nothing else was available.

Ames thinks he's a stud duck. To hear him talk, every woman in the county is just dying to impale herself on his magnificent penis. Oh, he gets his share all right. But he's not what you'd call particular. He used to have a girlfriend named Ruby who had a rear end the size of a number ten washtub. Ames didn't mind though. To him Ruby was special. "She likes to do it bent over," Ames said. "A lot of women won't let you do it that way. They're too bashful. But she likes it best that way."

Ames took a pull off his bottle. He kept talking. "She had these great big titties," he said, "and the only place she could find a bra to fit her was at a store over in Lepanto. I was there buying razors one day and had an idea to surprise her with a new bra. But I didn't know what size she took. When the saleslady asked me I just stuck my hands out two feet in front of me and said, 'About this size.' She went into the storeroom and came back with an outfit the size of a mule harness. I said, 'That looks like it'll fit,' and by God it did fit, too!" Ames took another drink. He was drinking it down pretty fast. "We went together for twenty-one years," he said. "She knew I wouldn't divorce Dolly so she started going out with this farmer. Before long he asked her to marry him. She came to me and said, 'Daddy, should I get married?' I said, 'Yes, if you can get a man who'll pay off your place and take care of you.' But all she got was a shit-ass. He spends her money and treats her terrible. She still tells me 'I love you, Ames.' She'll tell you today she loves Ames Thacker."

The poor sot was on the verge of tears so I changed the subject by requesting a scalp massage. It's only fifty cents extra and wonderfully soothing, especially for the sphenoid nerve. I even let him sell me a tube of scalp oil. Not that I'm afraid of losing my hair, but with all the sun I get out here my scalp tends to dry out. No, baldness doesn't run in the family. The sole bald relative I can recall is Aunt Grace, and hers was not a natural baldness but the result of an overzealous beauty operator chemically frying the hair off her head during the course of a botched permanent. As for my father, he retained a healthy head of hair until the day he died. That was one of the few parts of his anatomy he did hold on to however. By the time we stuck him in the ground he was all stove up, having lost his toes, feet, and legs, in that order, to a creeping putrescence. When his feet began to mortify they swelled up like big balloons that looked like they would bust if you squeezed them. As a result of the surgeons' prunings Dad's last remains were rather on the scanty side. What was left to bury accounted for at most about two-thirds of the bodily equipment he entered the world with, and that figure doesn't even include his prostatectomy. But at least there was that much. They could have buried what was left of the two Crimmins brothers in a cigar box. One winter day they were thawing dynamite in hot sand by a fire in a cornfield and they let it heat a little too long. The blast blew them to atoms. The boys were jumbled up so bad the undertaker had to scoop them up with a snow shovel, and even then most of what he collected was just mud and cornstalks. He couldn't tell what belonged to who so he divided the debris between the two caskets and slapped Richard's name on one and Robert's on the other. No one felt too bad when they heard about the boys blowing themselves up. They had been responsible for a lot of mischief. On the Fourth of July they tied a live cat to a rope by its tail and ran it up the school flagpole, and on Easter Sunday they skinned a rabbit and nailed it to the church door. It was never proven, but they were widely held to be the ones who drove iron railroad spikes into the hip joints of three of Jake Hewlett's quarterhorses, which had to be destroyed afterward. Something was wrong with those boys. I hate to think what they were planning to do with all that dynamite.

I was sixteen when Dad's first adverse physical symptoms began to appear, mostly in the form of gouty feet and puffiness around his ankles. His golf game suffered terribly, in fact it went totally to hell. Some days he couldn't stand to play at all, and those were times of discord and fracas in our household because he relied upon golf to soothe the nerves that a week of business frustrations had jangled to pieces. The verdant greens, the lush fairways, even the tangled rough exuded a calming influence by the sheer force of their greenness. It was always my opinion that this gout and the complications that followed resulted from two distinct yet related causes. The first was Dad's excess of weight. He was too fat. Oh, he wasn't obscenely obese like our neighbor Mr. Hedrick, who weighed well over three hundred pounds and whose abdomen seemed to stretch from his kneecaps to his armpits. And the fat didn't look that bad on Dad because he was tall enough and broad-shouldered enough to carry it in a way that wasn't absolutely indecent. But still he weighed far too much. One hundred and ninety pounds would have looked about right on him and he weighed two hundred and sixty-five. Naked, his paunch protruded well beyond his pubis, his butt was broad and flabby, and his breasts hung slack and droopy like old Mrs. Naismith's, the cheerful hag who dispensed the stringy grease-soaked hamburgers that were the specialty of the Table Top Cafe. Doc Gleason told him he should lose weight because it was putting a strain on his heart, but Dad never listened to anyone's advice, especially a doctor's, especially if it had to do with food. More than anything on earth he loved to eat and he wasn't about to have his favorite pastime interfered with.

The second cause of Dad's problems was that he was terminally constipated. The man couldn't crap to save his life. He was stopped up like the U-joint in a lead drainpipe. For this state of affairs the fault lay not just in the quantity of food that traversed his gullet, which was prodigious, but the type. His diet was atrocious. Jellied pork heads and salted beef tongues were just two of the gummy delicacies he insisted on gluing his bowels shut with, and the rest of the menu he fed on would have constipated an elephant. But rather than do something sensible like change what he ate, Dad preferred to try to laxate his way out of his digestive paralysis. At one time or another he must have tried every purgative known to man, and none of them ever provided him with more than the most temporary relief. Blue Mass was a bust, Pluto Water gave him gas, and Ex-Lax, in spite of its pleasant chocolatey taste and excellent reputation, failed utterly. Even Newton's vaunted Fig-Paste, guaranteed not to scour or gripe but gently to school the bowels to work without a physic, churned futilely on his behalf. His persecuted intestines simply refused to budge. It was a pathetic thing to watch every morning as Dad, armed to the teeth with pills, potions, and tonics, trudged down the hallway toward the bathroom like Hercules to the Augean stables to endure yet another hour perched in furious vain striving upon the cold and pitiless porcelain of the family commode.

Naturally this lack of eliminatory success had other deleterious effects. In addition to gouty and swollen feet he developed a horrendous case of the piles. His poor sphincter, strained beyond the breaking point time and time again, required numerous surgical interventions simply to maintain its structural integrity. But the worst part of his condition was that it made him cranky as hell.

There's nothing like a good six- or seven-day sludge buildup in your guts to put you on the grouchy side of things, and Dad became well known for the blackness of his temper. His tantrums occurred with great frequency and as a result of these explosions our relationship became one of, at best, strained wariness. Over the years he and I butted heads for reasons as trivial as how high to trim the hedge, the proper manner of conducting oneself at the dinner table, and even the most beneficial and salutory hour for awaking from sleep, which according to Dad was as close as possible to the moment of the day's dawning. I myself have always preferred the period after midday as a rising time. By then the dust and detritus kicked up by the hordes of frenetic morning worshipers has settled down, and it is pleasant to sit in the afternoon sun and drink coffee while contemplating the adventures of the coming evening. But my father believed with a passion that any man worth his salt rose and began his working day at first light, a pernicious belief fostered no doubt by his Spartan and cruelly deprived farmland upbringing in which practically from the time he was able to crawl he was being rousted out of bed at daybreak to poison sorghum midges, birth calves, and plow, till, and furrow the one hundred and twenty hardpan acres, which only by dint of relentless and exhaustive cultivation yielded the meager harvest that allowed his family to emaciate at a rate slightly slower than their neighbors.

The most sustained episode of head-butting between my father and me took place when I reached the age of eighteen. The point in dispute this time was neither hedges nor mealtime etiquette but in fact was nothing less momentous than the decision that would determine the course of my future, and even whether I had one (my opinion) or not (increasingly, Dad's position). To the extent that I had even given it much thought up to that point I had simply assumed that after high school I would attend a university, get the usual schooling in philosophy, literature, and history—especially history; I'd always been fascinated by the deeds of great men, the appearances and disappearances of empires and peoples, wars, plagues, destruction, and rapine—then embark upon my Wanderjahre, traipsing across the planet from country to country, imbibing the lore and traditions of all the world's nations. I wanted to see France, where the people are gay and impulsive and fond of military decorations; Turkey, ancient invasion-swept land of hospitable hookah smokers; China, enigmatic home to indolent coolie and industrious mechanic alike; Hindustan, the Holy Land, the Spice Islands, the Orinoco, the Ob, the Nile, the Iriwaddy; all the exotic and faraway places an adventurous spirit could ever want to visit.

But to my father my idea seemed the height of folly. "You can't just exist," he said, "you have to accumulate!" He saw no profit in my studying history, except perhaps as a hobby, and the idea of me traveling around the world like a hobo practically made him ill. He had lived through depressions, recessions, panics, collapses, bank runs, bankruptcies, credit crunches, and absconsions, and along with a volcanic blood pressure and that intractable set of hemorrhoids they had left him with an almost religious belief that the only way to success and security in this life lay through the application of a rigorously developed plan of action performed with backbreaking toil and continuous effort, and that any other way of life would bring only poverty, humiliation, desolation, and death. Since he had ascertained from long observance that I was a dreamy and somewhat impractical child who tended not a little toward sloth and even wastrelcy, and since he was the person who was going to be footing the bill for my further education, it seemed only natural to him that he should determine what that training should be. He had therefore arranged for me to attend in the fall, under his auspices and with his financial backing, Quincy Commercial Institute, his alma mater, where I would spend the next few years absorbing the principles of business and accounting, so that in the near future I could return home and assume the exalted position of bookkeeper at the family enterprise, a large department store downtown on Main Street, which supplied sundries, dry goods, hardware, clothing, groceries, and shoes to the citizens of our little town.

This store was my father's monument. It was his pride and his legacy and it carried on its front in huge letters the hallowed family name: HANNON'S. It was an imposing edifice. An architect from Louisville had been hired to give the exterior the noble facade it deserved and he had certainly achieved his aim. Above the name, which was handsomely painted in black gilt-edged letters, was a finely wrought Greek pediment-style cornice, and from street level there rose four black cast-iron Corinthian columns which supported three eighteen-foot-high white brick arches, each of them giving access to one of the store's three front entrances.

The left-hand entrance brought the customer directly into the women's department, a vast and frilly space filled with chemises, girdles, and ready-to-wear, all under the jurisdiction of Mrs. Mims, a powerfully built woman who wore a back brace and looked like she could throttle the life out of you with one hand if she so desired. It always seemed a little incongruous to me to see her holding up lacy negligees or underpants for the ladies' inspection, but she knew her wares well and the fact that she resembled nothing so much as a lumberjack or oilfield roustabout didn't seem to bother her customers one bit.

The righthand entrance led into furniture and hardware, the domain of Mrs. Mims's husband, Babe Mims. Babe was even stouter than Mrs. Mims, and though the expression on his face seemed to indicate that he was a bit slow-witted, in fact just the opposite was true. Babe was the store hawkshaw. He could take one look at a person when they walked in the door and tell whether they were honest or not. He was the one who told Dad it was a mistake to hire Henry Gibbs, and when Henry left a trail of bad checks drawn on the store all the way from Little Rock to Kansas City, Babe was proved right.

The center entrance opened into menswear, presided over by Joe Borders, a dapper and perfumed little man with an ingratiating smile and sympathetic eyes. Joe was a great salesman. It was said he could sell a suit of clothes to a dead man and many times he did exactly that, it being the custom in those days for the bereaved family of even the most shabbily dressed farmer or day laborer to want to send them off to glory in a better suit than they ever wore in their lifetime. As a result the dead in our town usually were fitted out better than the living, and obtained credit on easier terms, too. Joe's talents were so overwhelming that everyone overlooked his occasional indiscretions at the Lion's Club dances, where he seemed unable when drunk to restrain himself from groping at young men's privates in the bathroom, a habit that cost him more than one black eye and busted lip.

Also working at the store was my brother Frank, who at the age of twenty-six had already been named store manager and promised to be an excellent one, if the twin traits of extreme anality and maddening fussiness over detail were any qualifications, and in the retail business they certainly are. Frank was married, had two children, was a member of the Rotary Club, served on the school board, and with his wife, Catherine, taught the Young Adults class at the Methodist Church. He was set for life. With all his talents however, Frank lacked certain other skills that were necessary for the successful running of the business, namely the ability to deal with numbers. He could look at a room full of merchandise and tell how much of it he could move, but if he was given the same information in numerical form he was totally lost at sea. That is where I entered the picture, at least in Dad's mind. I did have a good head for figures, and for my father's purposes that made me the perfect person to take the place of Miss Lizzie Rader, the ancient and arthritic spinster who had faithfully kept the books for thirty years and now wanted nothing more than to retire and devote the remainder of her days to soaking her aching hipbones in the boiling therapeutic mineral baths at Hot Springs. With a little luck and a few timely cortisone injections she thought she could hold out until my training was completed, and the transition could be accomplished smoothly. Together, Frank and I would then insure that Hannon's would continue to be a profitable enterprise long after Dad lay mouldering in the soggy ground of the cemetery out on Highway 28. I don't know why Dad cared what happened after he was dead, but some people do, and he was one of those people.

It was an excellent plan, except that I had no intention of spending the next fifty years of my life hunched over a set of ledgers with my eyeballs exploding out of their sockets just so that at the end of a long and odious calculation two columns of disparate figures would match precisely down to the last squirming penny. In fact it would have been hard to imagine an occupation that would have appealed to me less. And even if I had been crass enough to consider going away to Quincy and coming back to work at the store for a year or two just to accumulate a bankroll for my travels, I still wouldn't have done it because I couldn't stand working for Frank. Frank and I didn't get along. I'd never forgotten the time he took me along with him and Bert Murphy on a business trip when I was fourteen. I had never been to Memphis before, so while Frank and Bert conducted their business I spent the whole afternoon wandering around the wharves watching the barges and bargemen hustling about their tasks. I had a grand time just sitting on the dock eating the bananas I had bought off a boat in from New Orleans. But back at the hotel, after supper, Frank said he thought it was time I had a woman. That was fine with me, I thought it was time I had a woman, too. First, apparently, it was necessary to get me drunk. They poured liquor down my throat until I was stupefied, then dragged me out into the garish streets in search of a whorehouse. After what seemed like weeks they hauled me sideways up a staircase into a parlor where a bunch of women were sitting semiclothed on overstuffed chairs and sofas. With a minimum of consultation and haggling I was given into the custody of a looming rouged figure and led away to the slaughter.

The next thing I knew it was morning. I was back in our hotel room and Frank and Bert were standing by my bed looking very worried. They had bad news. It was real bad news, too, not just your run-of-the-mill "The boiler has exploded and burned down the orphanage!" bad news. They'd learned that the woman I had been with the night before was contaminated, and that meant I was contaminated, too. Contaminated! I had the contamination! Luckily there was a cure, they said, but they'd have to get it from a doctor. It was expensive and they didn't have enough money to spare to pay for it. Now I had fifty dollars Dad had given me to buy a new suit. I pondered this but it didn't take me long, when weighing the new suit in the scales against the eternal loss of my generative organ, whose abilities I had only lately in private practices begun to appreciate, to comprehend that the suit had better wait. In fact, the suit had no chance at all. They left with the fifty dollars, instructing me to wrap my tool in hot towels until their return.

What a woebegone lad I was then! For one night of pleasure, of which I hadn't the faintest memory, I had risked my entire future. I was repentful. I prayed to God to restore me to health, to inflict any punishment, however hideous, so long as it didn't have to do with my penis. But I was afraid the nature of my crime would occasion precisely that type of retribution, and I knew I deserved it. Fearfully I perused my tool. Its aspect was red, puffy, angry. It seemed to wag its fevered head at me in mute reproach. My balls were afflicted, too. The right one in particular was noticeably lopsided, and looked like it was about to be jettisoned. My head was splitting and my brain felt on fire. How quickly the illness was spreading! Would I go blind, too? I shed exhausted tears at my plight and from time to time examined my shrunken member. Hours went by, the time broken only by miserable bouts of the dry heaves. Finally I fell into a nightmarish sleep. Toward evening Frank and Bert returned full of merriment and woke me up. They were in stitches. The whole thing had been a hoax. I hadn't been with any woman at all, much less a diseased one. At the whorehouse I had passed out and slept like a lamb. Today they had used my fifty dollars for another spree and thought it was a grand joke. I had a different opinion of it. When I got home I told my father I had lost the fifty dollars and he said I'd have to wait until next year for a new suit.

The day after my graduation from high school Dad called me into the living room. He wanted me to tell him, in no uncertain terms, at that moment, on that day, whether I was going to accede to his wishes and matriculate at Quincy in the fall. I didn't have to hesitate for a second. I said, "No." Since this wasn't even remotely close to what he wanted to hear, he reacted by blowing his top. The scene that followed was rather distasteful. To make sure I understood what he thought of my decision he stood (he still had both legs, both feet and all ten toes at that time, and though the swelling was getting worse every day he could still rise to the occasion when required) in front of me and crawled my hump for fifteen minutes. Even then he didn't quit because he was in any danger of running out of material but only because I think he thought he might have a stroke if he kept on. He called me all the usual things fathers call their sons when they want to impress upon them how pale a shadow they cast in comparison to their progenitor, plus he threw in a few original epithets that he must have been saving up for just such an occasion. He was so inspired that I was hard pressed to find a point where I could mount a counterattack, and ultimately I gave up, figuring that since I was still hung over from the reveries of graduation night I wouldn't be as eloquent as I wanted to be anyway. I just stood there and took it, and when he got to the part where he said that if I didn't intend to go to Quincy I could get out of his house immediately, there was nothing to do but go to my room to pack my suitcase.

It is never a pleasant feeling to be expelled, whether from a movie theater for setting fire to the seats or from a library for farting too loudly in the reading room. And though I had tried to act so as not to betray the effect his words had on me, in fact I was pretty disturbed. I had spent the past eighteen years under that same roof, taking three meals a day, hauling away countless quantities of oak leaves from the yard every fall, and in my mind I felt I had accumulated some kind of rights, if not of ownership at least of habitation. Now these rights had been suddenly and unilaterally terminated, and the more I thought about it the more it burned me up. As I packed I became increasingly peeved, until before I knew it I was ready to make someone pay for the harsh insult I had suffered. My imagination turned to all sorts of patricidal scenarios, from emptying all six bullets from his service revolver into Dad's overfed stomach while he was bingeing at the breakfast table, to marching down Main Street in front of Hannon's Department Store with the old man's head impaled on a bloody spike. For the first time in my life I felt like I could really and truly appreciate the story of Oedipus. It makes so much sense! If some evil s.o.b. pierces your ankles, hands you over to a shepherd, and orders you placed on a barren mountainside to be devoured by wolves, what recourse do you have other than to hunt the bastard down and beat him to death with a rake? And as for fucking your mother, what harm is there in that, really, seeing as how your father is dead already anyway?

Thoughts of this sort dominated my thinking for a good half

an hour. But as I was still rather young in a lot of respects, and hadn't yet learned how to cultivate a truly sustainable hatred, by the time I got down to choosing which extra pair of shoes to take with me my anger was already turning into sadness, an infinite sadness borne of the revelation that this might be the last time I would ever see the inside of the room that had nurtured and consoled me for all the past six thousand six hundred some-odd days of my life. More and more mournfully I looked around those four walls, and everywhere I looked I saw the tokens of my childhood: my snake-skins hanging above the radiator; my marbles filling two full half-gallon milk bottles; my Confederate twenty-dollar bill carefully encased behind a glass picture frame. A wave of grief swept over me as the memories came rushing back. How could I leave the room where my pet turtle had starved to death? The room where a legion of goldfish had swum into oblivion in the murky water of the fishbowl on top of my dresser? The room whose walls and ceiling had witnessed and even encouraged my first furtive and hysterical copulations with a pillow? It was too sad for words. Tears came to my eyes, and I tried in vain to suppress the sobs welling up in my chest.

But before long these feelings also began to mutate, into something that at least approximated resolve, or gumption, or some of the other manly qualities I had been accused only half an hour before of not possessing. It was time to go. I closed the door to my room and began the long journey that would lead me out of the house, pausing only long enough to make a quick detour into Dad's bedroom. There I hastily dug through his sock drawer and removed several objects I thought I might need, among them his hunting knife, his pistol, most of his prophylactics, and his treasured deck of nude playing cards featuring fifty-four (counting the jokers) of the finest burlesque queens the South had to offer. After stashing this booty in my bag I made my way to the kitchen, opened the screen door, went onto the back porch, wiped my feet on the welcome mat, and stepped out into the heavy humid air of a deepening June evening, vowing never to return.

My new home was a room in Mrs. Naylor's boardinghouse, a tilting ramshackle three-story wreck of a building that occupied most of a narrow dirt plot a half block away from the business district. Mrs. Naylor's establishment wasn't the kind of place you would expect to find a young person taking up residence. Except for the occasional traveling salesman or railroad section gang passing through for the night, most of the inhabitants were well into their dotage and lived on a variety of means almost exclusively related to pensions, retirement funds, or outright donations from the state. The room on one side of me was occupied by Mr. Louis Leclerc, an eighty-two-year-old retired army sergeant who represented the tail end of four generations of distinguished military service, including a grandfather who had been crucified on an anthill by a band of Oglala Sioux he had somehow managed to offend. The cavalry cutlass of this martyred ancestor was displayed prominently above the mantelpiece in Mr. Leclerc's room. My other neighbor was Mrs. Delpha Tollner, a retired Sunday School teacher who lived with her daughter Imogene, who was a disabled nurse, and their pet parakeet, Petey, a green and yellow fiend who loved nothing better than to swoop down from his perch hidden in the folds of the draperies to try and peck out the eyes of unsuspecting visitors. Mrs. Tollner was fiercely proud of the fact that in fifty-seven years of teaching Sunday School only two of her more than six hundred students had wound up in correctional facilities. "And that Biggers boy wasn't your fault, Mother," Imogene said, inhaling adrenaline from a glass pipe she smoked twice a day for her asthma. "He was a little dickens from the start."

The lodgings left something to be desired. My abode had crumbling wallpaper, a ceiling that was a growing sea of ancient and recent water stains, and woodwork charred and blackened from a fire caused by the previous tenant's malfunctioning hotplate. The furniture consisted of a couple of sagging iron bedsteads, a rickety shambles of a chifforobe, and a cracked cold-water sink that threatened to riot off its pipes whenever the water was turned on and probably would have if not for a jerry-rigged system of two-by-fours and electrical wire that held it straitjacketed to the wall. And the atmosphere wasn't always as serene as one might expect. Mrs. Naylor's son Anthony was a somewhat menacing figure who roamed the halls at night in his underwear and could be seen standing on the porch fondling his genitals behind the screen door as he watched teenage girls walk past on their way downtown after school. As I learned later, Tony, a bona fide electronic genius, was subject to frequent bouts of mental disturbance caused by a hormonal imbalance, and even after years of treatment for his psychological problems still continued his unfortunate habit of eating his food out of tin cans and then reusing them to store his bodily wastes in. Thankfully the door to his room was always closed. There was also a running feud between the Tollners and Mr. Leclerc. The two ladies wouldn't speak to him in the hall and refused to sit anywhere near him at meals. According to them he was lucky they hadn't had him arrested, for making what they claimed were "improper advances" to Imogene in the tub room. When I asked Mr. Leclerc about it he became indignant. He said it was a preposterous idea that he would make an advance of any kind, even a proper one, toward Imogene. He said the whole thing was the result of an egregious error on his part. He had gone to the tub room without his glasses, and seeing someone he took to be the maid bent over cleaning the bathtub he had playfully grabbed her around the waist from behind, an embrace that sent the startled Imogene shrieking down the hall. "Look at Imogene," he said in his defense. "If I had been seeing straight there's no way in hell I would have done anything but bugle retreat!"

The room was small and crummy, but it was cheap, and this was important because money was in short supply. I had a little saved up from working afternoons at the store, but that wasn't going to last long. The first thing I did was to go to work for Ben Foster at the bowling alley. I'd worked there in the past, and I was good at it. Terry Coleman said I was the best pin-setter he'd ever seen, and he'd always roll a silver half-dollar down the lane to me when his frames were done. Ten-pin, nine-pin, cocked hat, I put the pins down fast and perfectly placed every time. But there wasn't much money in pin-setting. The most I ever made was the time Allen Pryor paid me ten dollars to help him win a twenty-dollar bet against Stu Larkin. Stu was Allen's boss. They always came in to bowl on their lunch hour and Stu always won. This time though, I set the headpin a fraction of an inch in front of where it should have been, so that the pins didn't go down for Stu the way they usually did. When Allen won Stu couldn't believe it. He had never lost to Allen in his life.

To supplement my income I also started helping my friend Matt Moore with his moonshine business. Matt and I had known each other since birth and on many occasions we had risked our fate together in enterprises involving varying degrees of criminality, from the relatively minor vandalism of uprooting all the sweet corn in Mrs. Taylor's vegetable garden, to the grand larceny reflected in the cumulative theft of literally hundreds of dollars worth of fishing tackle from Bateman's Bait shop. Old Man Bateman only had one good eye, so all you had to do was wait until it was turned toward the wall behind the register and then you could stuff all the lures, reels, and tackle you wanted down the front of your britches.

Since our county was dry a lot of people preferred to buy local homemade products rather than drive fifty miles for legal liquor, and Matt did a brisk business fulfilling this need. His supplier was Woodenhead Wieger, who had a still out on Cypress Creek. It was the best stuff around. It was naturally brown because it was cured in charcoal in an oak barrel buried in Woodenhead's backyard. Matt and I would drive out to Woodenhead's in Matt's father's hearse, buy four or five gallon jugs and head back to the funeral parlor, where we pulled into the garage to transfer the gallons into pints and half-pints. A hickory shad half-pint sold for seventy-five cents, a pint for a dollar and a quarter. Once I sold seventeen half-pints in half an hour in the alley behind the movie theater. With sales like that we could double our money in two days.

Although these arrangements solved my money worries for the time being, there was another problem that wasn't so easily taken care of, and this was the fact that my fiancée wasn't very happy about any of these recent developments in my life. Sarah had a profoundly healthy disgust for the squalor I was living in at Mrs. Naylor's, and she also didn't trust my association with Matt, who she felt was going to get me into trouble. She couldn't fathom why I didn't just accept my father's offer, with its promise of financial security, and settle down to fulfill my true destiny, which was to marry her. Sarah wasn't really my fiancée, at least not in any official capacity yet, but in her mind this was just a technicality that she anticipated being rectified any day now. To her way of thinking, she and I had been going out for a year and a half and that could only mean one thing: next stop, the altar. In this she was no different from any of the other girls in town. They all thought if you got hold of a boyfriend and were letting him have some goober on a regular basis that entitled you to a wedding. It was practically guaranteed in the Constitution. This meant a guy had to be careful, because some of the more desperate ones thought nothing of springing a fetus on you to persuade you to walk them down the aisle. It very nearly happened to Matt once. A little sweet-faced girl with delicate hands who worked at the telephone company had Matt over to her house a few times and told him to forget about using a rubber, she liked it raw. She said she had a high-powered wash that would fix things up afterward. But about a month later she came by the funeral home and told Matt she was pregnant. When he didn't say anything she said, "Doesn't that mean anything to you?" Matt said, "Yeah, doctors' bills and the end of my hard-on." He went to Doc Gleason, who told him, "I wouldn't believe too much of that if I were you." Doc was right. There was nothing to it. But it shook Matt up.

Marriage fever was running high that year all over town. The spring had been a veritable hotbed of nuptial activity, with engagements and weddings popping up week after week like mushrooms in cow patties. Sarah got caught up in the general stampede and couldn't think about anything else. It was partly my fault for not putting a stop to it sooner, but I didn't take it seriously at first. When I would go over to her house and find her in her room mooning over photographs of bridal gowns and accessories in the women's magazines I just thought to myself, "These are harmless fantasies. Let her indulge them." And when she served as a bridesmaid in three of her friends' weddings I not only encouraged her but even pronounced her lovely and charming in the farcical outfits the occasions required. It wasn't until I became aware that she was spending every waking hour reading subversive manuals with titles like *The Pleasures of Betrothal* and *The Little House for Two* that I realized how far gone she was, and by then it was too late. I found out that a lot of other people in town shared her ideas. When I went into the jewelry store to pick up my watch from being repaired, Mrs. Castor smiled and asked me if I would be coming in soon to pick out a ring. And Mr. Pearson at the furniture store told me he had a beautiful bedroom suite on sale that he would hold for me until I had a chance to look it over. It almost seemed like a conspiracy among the merchants. I could see how they set their sights on a likely young couple, talked it up among themselves, spread the word around town, got the girl's mother all excited and let her run with the ball, and the next thing you know the girl herself is enflamed and the church is reserved and the jewelers and caterers and florists start making plans to take vacations, buy new cars, and redecorate their living rooms with the ill-gotten gains they have bamboozled out of the couple's families, whom they have by now convinced that unless they rent the antique cut-glass epergne, the gilded flower trellis, *and* the brass candelabra the entire function will be considered a dismal failure.

Well, I didn't intend to be the dupe of their little schemes. From my vantage point getting married right out of high school seemed like the worst kind of trap there was. There was no dearth of instructive examples, the most recent being the marriage of my seventeen-year-old cousin Bethel Turner to Darnell Slakes, who had knocked her up. Even in that condition the family would have preferred to endure the ignominy of an illegitimate birth rather than have to accept the likes of Darnell into their home, but Bethel thought she was in love and was determined to have a husband. The Slakeses were all for it, too. No Slakes within living memory had held a steady job and the idea of Darnell getting his hooks into Bethel's father's lucrative lumberyard business had the entire Slakes clan slobbering and yipping like a pack of blind dogs running loose in a meathouse. The whole thing was a fiasco. In his glee at his prospects Darnell had stayed up the better part of three days engaged in a ritualistic drinking orgy, and by two o'clock that Saturday afternoon he could do little more than wobble around in the front of the church like a seasick chimpanzee. The rest of the Slakes folk were also in a extremely intoxicated state. They practically had a party going on in the first three pews, carousing and laughing and just having a grand old time. Things were more somber on the other side of the aisle. Bethel's relations looked totally disgusted and appalled at having to be in the presence of such trash, and the way Bethel's mother was sobbing and carrying on you would have thought she was at a funeral. All that was missing was the coffin. Meanwhile at the back of the church you could hear Mr. Turner and Bethel shouting at each other, he saying it wasn't too late for her to call the whole thing off and trundle out to Montana to her aunt's house to deliver the little bundle of joy there, and she saying it was her wedding day and she goddamned well was going through with it and if he wasn't such a miserable penny-pinching tightwad who never wanted her to have anything nice for herself he would realize how important it was to her and shut up. This argument carried on right up to the moment when Mrs. Caswell launched into her massacre of the wedding march. Bethel practically had to drag her father down the aisle behind her to take her place next to Darnell, who kept turning his head sideways to mug and wink at his drooling family. The preacher whipped through the ceremony in under two minutes. No one fainted, but Darnell's brother Lester did manage to throw up into the little flower girl's bouquet. I imagine she developed some of the same sentiments about weddings as I did. Things didn't get any better at the reception. Mrs. Turner still couldn't stop sobbing so Mr. Turner had her tranquilized and put to bed, causing her to miss the cutting of the cake, a five-tiered monstrosity with tiny voodoo fetishes of the happy couple on top. After a few hours of eats and toasts and more toasts, with some additional ad hoc vomiting by other members of the groom's party, Bethel and Darnell were packed off in Bethel's father's car and sent away on a weekend honeymoon at Table Rock Lake. By Monday morning they were back home ensconced in a house rented for them by Mr. Turner, and from that day on were embroiled in a neverending nightmare of missed insurance payments, installment-bought furniture, and every twisted and maddening sort of obligation to relatives that you can imagine.

No, I had loftier goals than getting stuck in that kind of a bog, and it was probably in response to my fear of finding myself caught in just such a situation that I had recently thrust myself into an even more perilous quagmire, one that presented the very real possibility that a man named Wayne Slavings might any day now be coming to kill me for having an affair with his wife. Wayne was a tough hombre, a rough, rowdy shit-kicking tugboat hand best known in our community for his fight with Alvin Bowers that destroyed the interior of the American Legion Hall. The two men had slugged it out for over half an hour, smashing chairs into splinters and windows into glass dust, until one of them heaved a Civil War–era relic cannonball into the fusebox and the lights went out. The fight could have ended right then, but Jum Jenkins drove his jeep up the front steps and shone the headlights inside so they could keep at it. They managed to break every stick of furniture in the place and all the glasses and pool cues to boot before Alvin went down for the count with a skull fracture, a lacerated kidney, and fifteen broken teeth. Since Wayne only got himself a busted cheek, a sprained ankle, and seven cracked knuckles he was regarded as the definite winner.

I knew better than to get involved with Rachel Slavings, but I just couldn't resist the temptation. She was twenty-five, had long black hair, green eyes, and more curves than the logging road around Big Beaver Mountain. Our acquaintance had begun innocently enough one day when she came into the store shopping for curtains. While she was examining some bolts of muslin we got into a conversation, and after that whenever she came in we'd talk, either in the shoe department, or in appliances, or especially over by yard tools, where we could have a little more privacy. One day I was telling Rachel about the parties some of my friends and I had been having out at the railroad trestle, and she said she'd like to go to one. Now these parties weren't much of anything really, just five or six of us guys driving out to the river, getting crazy on bootleg liquor, then driving back into town whooping and hollering and shouting, "We eat pussy!" at carloads of out-of-town girls. It really wasn't the kind of function to take a date to. But Rachel said she wanted to see the trestle, so one Monday night when Wayne was away I arranged to borrow Matt's car and met Rachel in the alley a block from her house.

There wasn't a party that night, just the two of us there. And there was nothing too remarkable about the trestle. It was just an old rusted steel structure over the Willow River. But it was twenty feet above the water, there was an eerie swamplike atmosphere to the place, and it felt scary and risky to walk out to the middle of the thing and think about the Cotton Belt Express coming around the curve at fifty miles an hour, giving you the choice either to try to outrun it to the other end or jump feet first into the dark and snake-infested current below. We parked, walked onto the trestle looking at the stars and listening to the cries of nightbirds, then stopped in the middle to kiss on the crossties. We did that for a while. Then we walked with our arms around each other to the hearse, where we climbed in the back and lay down on a quilted coffin cover Matt kept inside for just such a circumstance. We were out there a long time, parked in the lee of the railroad embankment, I think it was about three hours. When it got to be two o'clock we left. I drove Rachel back to town, dropped her off, and went home. It was a good beginning, and we didn't stop there. Wayne's work on the river kept him gone for three weeks at a time, so Rachel and I were able to meet late at night virtually without impediment, and even without very much trepidation.

But the first time Wayne came home that bubble of semi-serenity burst. Wayne Slavings up close was a terrifying sight. His face and neck were highlighted with knife scars, part of his nose was missing (slashed off), his teeth (the ones he had left) looked like he had filed them down to sharp points, and he had two thumbs on his left hand. It was really just one thumb, with a sort of second demithumb sprouting out of it midway up its length between the base and knuckle. Still it was a pretty impressive deformity, and when he used it as a bridge for his pool cue, sliding the cue in the natural crook heredity had provided him with, he was a dead shot. I kept my distance in the pool hall, watching from the back wall as Wayne took on a series of past and future penitentiary dwellers (even Mrs. Tollner could have done nothing for this crew), and it didn't take me long to convince myself that it was ruinous to indulge an infatuation with the wife of a man who if he found out would certainly feel obligated to at least permanently disfigure me, if not kill me outright. And I didn't have a doubt in the world that Alvin Bowers would second my thoughts on the subject. After considering all the angles, I decided that my future health and well-being depended upon my not seeing Rachel again, and I swore I would give her up and stay close to Sarah, whose innocent concern over my increasing state of exhaustion—she insisted that I be tested for mononucleosis, which I did do, and that I try to get more sleep, which I did not do—was really quite touching.

Yet as soon as Wayne left again for the river I found that my terror subsided, my caution vanished, and my resolutions went the way of all weak flesh. Once more I was borrowing Matt's car to cruise the alleys behind Rachel's house, waiting for her with the lights off, and slipping out of town by the side streets into the countryside. The only concession I made to my fear was to drive deeper into the swamp. I felt safer there, on a weed-covered road that ran alongside the railroad tracks to an abandoned sawmill, where the only sounds aside from the passing midnight train were screech owls or the occasional wildcat scream, a cry that sounded unnervingly similar to the travails of a person being hacked to death with a dull ax. There Rachel and I spent our nighttime hours curled together in the back of the hearse until two or three in the morning, oblivious to doom, practically begging the Fates to strike us down. And if there is one thing about the Fates that is certain, it is that they wish for nothing more than to strike people like us down, and it takes a very minimal amount of begging to get them to do it.

For six weeks after my expulsion I didn't speak a word to my father. Oh, I saw him around. He was impossible to miss. I usually saw him hobbling downtown toward the store on his swollen feet with his cane, trying to accomplish by this minimal form of exercise what he should have accomplished with a diet. A couple of times I saw him coming out of the Tax Assessor's office, smoking a big cigar. I figured that meant he'd just gotten a blow job from his mistress, Lettie Gillis, who worked there. This was pure speculation on my part. It's highly doubtful they could accomplish anything of a sexual nature in that place, what with Lettie having to answer calls from irate tax payers every fifteen seconds. But the affair itself wasn't in doubt. When I was going through Dad's dresser drawers I'd found a metal Trojan container wrapped in a tissue with a lipstick print on it and the initials L. G. written in a red scrawl. And even more convincingly, Allen Gillis, Lettie's son, had told Dave Nichols that he and Barry Ritter had hidden under his mother's bed one night when they knew my father was coming over and had aurally witnessed the entire act. I thought it was an amazingly courageous and perverted thing to do, and even years later when Allen grew up to be a mean and nasty adult who liked to take puppies out into the countryside, set them running, and use them for moving target practice with his .22, I still maintained a certain appalled admiration for the thirteen-year-old boy who had possessed such daring.

Various attempts were made to reconcile us. Every few days my mother dropped off tins of cookies or brownies at Mrs. Naylor's with little notes inside begging me to come home. Mrs. Mims, Babe, and Joe Borders all buttonholed me on the street at one time or another and started waxing nostalgic about the past, reminding me that I'd practically grown up inside that store playing in the nail bins, flinging myself into the huge coils of heavy rope kept in the basement and getting sick on the stick candy I pilfered from the jars behind the cash register. My brother's wife, Catherine, tried to smooth things over by inviting Sarah and me to dinner, and after Frank apologized for having threatened to hit me over the head with a milk bottle a few weeks before—I'd stopped by his house early one morning to drop off some inventory calculations I'd done for him before I quit, and when Frank saw me coming he picked up the milk bottle off the back porch and said, "I've got a notion to knock you in the head with this." I said, "You've got another notion that beats the hell out of that one," and turned around and left—Catherine came up with the idea that as a compromise perhaps I could study a subject I liked, but that would also have some practical application. "What about agriculture?" she said. Dad owned some farm land that needed to be managed. Maybe I would like to try my hand at that. This wasn't a totally ridiculous notion, because in fact at one point I had considered pursuing that kind of career. My sophomore year I had even joined the Future Farmers of America and taken a class called "Modern Methods of Poultry Production," which emphasized the application of scientific hygiene to the raising of chickens. We cleaned cages, measured egg dimensions, and weighed hens, entering our observations in a log book. We delved into the latest studies in genetics and learned to what degenerative depths this once proud and vigorous breed of wildfowl has sunk: how inbreeding and poor selection have led to a loss of vitality, sluggishness of temperament, suspension of the maternal instinct, and other horrors; how a deplorable craze for ornamental heavy feathering has resulted in vastly lower egg production. Our efforts were concentrated on the Leghorn and the Plymouth Rock, two rather unglamorous but sturdy breeds that enjoy well-deserved reputations as superior egg producers. The only allowance to exoticism was a single phlegmatic Buff Orpington, a striking yet practical breed resulting from the careful crossbreeding of a Golden Spangled Hamburg, a Buff Cochin, and a Dark Dorking. It was all a far cry from the type of chicken farming I was familiar with. The fellow Dad had looking after his chickens, who we knew only by the name of Donk, didn't give a thought to the chickens' hygiene, and why should he, when his own house resembled a pig sty? His yard was filled with junked refrigerators and ovens and the chickens roosted and dropped their eggs wherever they pleased. A favorite place was beneath the rusted hulk of what was once an automobile and was now the abode of slithery creatures, with tall weeds sprouting from the tailpipe and a volunteer walnut sapling springing up stout and ineradicable right through the cracked engine block. Donk left the actual collecting of the meager egg yield to the members of his family. That gave him more time to devote to his drinking, an occupation which took up most of his waking hours and barely left him enough time to beat his wife and children before they went to sleep. Donk was the source of much arcane knowledge, like if you slaughtered a calf in the new moon and found blood clotted in its haunches, we were in for a dry spell. He had more in common with insects and animals than with other human beings, and spent his few active hours examining raccoon tracks, woolly worms, and locust shells for portents. In spite of these formidable abilities Dad finally had Donk and his family evicted from the farmhouse. They left a mess. The floor was covered with filthy newspapers and rags, and we discovered to our chagrin that they had spent the winter crapping in the closet instead of using the outhouse. I didn't blame them. Who wants to brave freezing temperatures and biting winds just to have your buttocks stick to a frozen and splintery outhouse seat? Under those circumstances, shitting in the closet has a certain irresistible attraction. But Dad was disgusted. The only sympathy he expressed was for their dog. He felt like he owed it an apology for having to live with such bestial people.

The sole person who hadn't tried to influence me was my grandfather. Grandpa said, "Go ahead, live like a bum if you want to. I spent some of the best years of my life as a bum. I rode a train from here to California with only a quarter in my pocket and a jar of baked potatoes to eat. When I got home six months later I still had the quarter but my own mother didn't even recognize me. She made me undress outside the house and then she burned my clothes."

But Grandpa wasn't in such good shape. He had some kind of throat affliction that made it so hard to swallow that he'd usually lose patience halfway through a meal and throw his plate across the room. Then he'd shout, "Goddamn! Goddamn!" until his cook, Nola, came in and cleaned up the mess. There was also something wrong with his wiener, which by now had been reduced to a leaky purple hose that hung down uselessly between his legs. He was constantly getting probed and reamed up at the clinic, and what I overheard there cured me forever of wanting to live to be old:

"I just had my neck artery cleaned out. It was eighty-five percent plugged up and I was just on the border of a seizure."

"How'd they catch it? You have light fainting spells or something?"

"No, I got sick to my stomach and couldn't keep my equilibrium. I've got to have the other one done now. Before that I had my gall bladder surgery and now I've got to see if my kidneys need flushing. How's your husband?"

"They had to bring him back in. He had that prostate operation and started hemorrhaging and developed blood clots. He passed ten clots in one night. Then his heart started backing up on him. He was about to have knee surgery when he came up with that prostate. They put the knee off till this fall. How's your brother doing?"

"It was cancer. They had to remove his testicles and now they're giving him radiation treatments."

That's when I'd go outside and wait on the sidewalk. After a while Grandpa would come out cursing the bastards who'd hogtied him, thrown him on a tabletop, and stuck something that looked like a seedhorn up his butt for half an hour. He'd bitch all the way home, then start yelling at Nola for overcooking the ham hocks. Grandpa knew he was a goner, but he kept things in perspective. "I still like it here," he said, "but I can't last much longer."

The fact is, I *was* living like a bum. The accommodations at Mrs. Naylor's were just short of being condemned (I don't mean to denigrate my neighbors, because in spite of the reduced circumstances they lived in Mrs. Tollner and Imogene always carried themselves with a certain panache, Mrs. Tollner always appearing at meals coiffed in one of her many wigs and Imogene looking very stylish with her six-inch cigarette holder and colorful bandannas. Even Mr. Leclerc managed to maintain a certain dignity about his person), and a lot of the people I was hanging around with were lowlifes, like Waymon Lufford, the local arsonist who personally was responsible for the conversion of innumerable houses, warehouses, and businesses from unsalable real estate into cold hard insurance company cash, or Clifford Sandifer, a shade-tree mechanic (when he worked at all) who was always quick to let you know, in case you were somehow randomly wondering about it or had perhaps heard something to that effect, that he had never in his life had intercourse with any kind of farm animal, though if he got drunk enough he would eventually acknowledge that he might have assisted in holding down one of Bobby Dabney's DuRoc sows late one spring evening while Bobby pressed his loins against the unfortunate porker. But the difference, as I saw it, was that I didn't plan to stay in this milieu of house burners and pig fuckers all my life, or even very much longer. In my mind, I was just marking time until September, when I fully expected to be sitting in a classroom reading Caesar's "The War in Gaul," or Herodotus's "Histories", or examining in detail the events leading to the invasion of Portugal by Spain in 1763, a ridiculously flawed campaign in which the Spanish general, after spending six months trying to engage in battle the wily and undermanned Portuguese army whose sole talent in warfare consisted of their skill in retreating, finally declared, "I cannot find where these insects are!" and turned around and went back home. I don't know why I continued to think, as June passed into July and July passed into August without any sign of a crack in my father's resolve and I began to worry that possibly I had overplayed my hand, that Dad would eventually give in and let me do what I wanted to do. There certainly was no precedent for such a reversal in our family's history. Yet that was what I was expecting to happen.

During this time Sarah, either because she was utterly submerged in her bridal revelries or because she was concentrating all her efforts on determining which argument was most likely to succeed in getting me to change my mind about going to Quincy, hadn't voiced any suspicions about my rather negligent behavior, other than to accuse me once of sneaking around to see Sissy Hardwick, who I used to date before Sarah and I got together. But that was an all-purpose standing accusation she trotted out whenever she wanted to stir things up, and when I denied it she backed off almost immediately and was even somewhat apologetic while she went around the room picking up the pieces of the footstool she'd shattered against the wall during our discussion. But she had still continued to hector me about setting a date to announce our engagement, and recently she had even hinted that if I didn't want to marry her there were plenty of guys who did. By "plenty of guys" she was referring to Calvin Lucas, the geekish son of the Methodist preacher, who was always lurking around looking for a way to get in good with her. Calvin was a twit. When he first moved to town and was looking to find a girlfriend we'd told him that Martha Hopper was interested in him. We pointed her out to him on the street and said that she lived outside of town and was dying for him to come and see her. So he dressed up in a nice pair of pants and a white shirt and Will Barnes said he'd drive him out and introduce him. In the meantime we all drove out in another car to the house of Gary Sauger, who Calvin didn't know yet. Gary met us there with a shotgun loaded with blanks. We all went inside to wait, and pretty soon Will drove up to the house with Calvin. They both got out of the car and walked up to the door together and were just about to knock when Gary threw open the door and leveled the shotgun on them. "So you're the sons of bitches that have been banging my daughter!" he yelled, and he aimed the shotgun right at Will's chest and fired. Will fell to the ground like he had been shot and screamed, "He's done got me, Calvin, save yourself!" Calvin took off across the yard like a cat with the bloody flux and Gary fired off the other barrel to get him running even a little faster. Calvin hit the barbed wire fence broadside, flipped over it, got up, and started running again, leaving half his pants hanging on the wire. When he got back to the pool hall we were all waiting for him. He didn't hang out with us much after that.

Perhaps I should have been concerned about Sarah getting fed up, but I was so busy sneaking around with Rachel that I didn't give it any thought. It didn't even occur to me as a possibility. Rachel and I had been gallivanting all over the area, using a series of secluded parking spots, from the gravel road leading to the city dump where Matt and I used to take potshots at tin cans and brown rats with our BB guns, to a dead-end dirt track up on Neville's Ridge, an anomalous geologic feature in this region of lowlands, from where we had a long-distance view of the lights of solitary farmhouses, and could hear the distant whoosh of cars going flat-out down the steep slope of the ridge highway in the still time after midnight. Once we even ventured out before dark, driving to Gradyville one late afternoon to watch the sun go down over Eleven Mile Slough, a picturesque little venue of swampish muck and cypress trees that was positively aflutter with all kinds of bird life, including two mated white swans that had somehow managed to avoid being mink food for the past three or four seasons they had nested there. It was extremely romantic, with the sun sinking in the west and the full moon rising in the east up over the cattail flags while a soft breeze was blowing off the water, but it was risky to go there and chance being seen, and we knew it and we still did it. We were acting as if Wayne didn't exist at all, as if we could do whatever we wanted with impunity, and the thrill of the danger made it even more exciting. The only time reality intruded upon my consciousness during this period was, paradoxically, when I was unconscious. Then the danger seemed all too real. At least once a week I would wake up from a nightmare in a cold sweat, having just experienced the utter terror of seeing Wayne coming at me with a butcher knife, or brass knuckles, or an icepick, or even his bare fists, and no matter how many streets I ran down or how many doors I shut behind me he would still pop up right in front of me, ready to kick my ass. If I had been paying attention maybe I would have taken these dreams as warnings, but in my state of insouciance probably no warning would have sufficed, because the impulses directing me toward disaster were simply too strong.

Ames's father Beryl used to have a barbershop at the north end of Independence Street, with three chairs and a collection of rotting taxidermized animals on the walls, including a specimen he invented himself that consisted of a rooster's head stuck on a baby alligator's body, which he claimed was an animal called a "roostigator." Only small children and a few virtual morons actually believed it was a real creature. Between the leaky sawdust and the fact that Beryl chewed tobacco that he spit in the sink while he was cutting your hair, the shop was just about completely filthy. It was while sitting there in that barbershop, surrounded by the usual aggregation of geezers, peach fuzzes, and just plain old farts waiting to get their ears lowered, that I got the first indication that I might be in some serious trouble with Wayne Slavings.

It was a Saturday, the last day of the Homecoming Festival, which was held every year the first week in August. This was a four-day-long celebration that consisted of a carnival, a parade, a tractor and farm implement exhibition, livestock judging, beauty contests, and nightly performances of a Passion Play depicting the last days of Jesus leading up to his crucifixion, a droll little entertainment that was put on by a cast made up of every species of Baptist in existence in our area: Southern Baptists, Missionary Baptists, First General Baptists, Second General Baptists, Willow River Baptists, Mount of Olives Baptists (who either by choice or as a punishment or perhaps simply by tradition were always told to provide a Pontius Pilate) and Free Will Baptists. They always threw in a Methodist or a Presbyterian or two in the name of ecumenicality, but basically the play was a Baptist production through and through. They had been putting the thing on for twenty-seven years and by virtue of repetition it had become a regional tradition that drew people from all over that section of the country.

Contrary to the faithful's purpose in presenting their little drama, a good number of churchgoers had come to regard the festivities of Homecoming Weekend as providing an exemption from their church's usual prohibitions against alcohol, and in fact it seems the stricter their particular denomination's condemnation of drinking, the more they were hellbent on doing it. The result was that the Homecoming Festival had become a bonanza for the moonshine sellers. The last day of the Festival was the single greatest selling day of the year, because that was the day when all the forty-acre farmers and sharecroppers and hired hands left their squalid little shotgun shacks and flooded the town with their rattling pickups overloaded with harelipped children and weatherbeaten wives, which they deposited at the carnival before proceeding to buy some hooch downtown and get stinking drunk. In anticipation of huge sales Matt had laid in extra stores from Woodenhead, about twelve gallons' worth, and after breaking the gallons down to pints and mixing in some embalming fluid (a recent development in the moonshine trade in our county, and not necessarily a good one, had been the addition of liquids like paint thinner or wood alcohol or other additives to the local products to give them more kick. Matt and I hadn't wanted our stuff to compare unfavorably with these high octane brews, so to be on the safe side we had begun adding a pint and a half of embalming fluid to every gallon of ruckus juice, to make our brand at least as fiery as everybody else's) we went off downtown to start selling.

We sold to everybody. Farmers, teachers, pharmacists, church deacons, you name it, they came slinking out the back entrances of stores or nonchalantly appeared at the head of the alley, acting as though they had nothing on their minds but a pleasant stroll, and then they would sidle up behind the meat market incinerator and follow us to the loading dock of the Post Office, where we would sell them what they wanted. Benton Linn, vice-president of the bank, bought a pint, and so did Tommy Hughes, the municipal judge. I even sold a pint to my brother Frank who, because of his excessive self-consciousness about his civic standing, sent Clyde Mills the delivery man to buy it. By five o'clock in the afternoon we had completely sold out of our stock on hand. Since there wouldn't be any more until after Woodenhead had finished the late afternoon run of his still, we quit for the time being and split up because Matt had to go back to the funeral home to help his father burn some baby caskets. Fifteen years before, one summer when babies were succumbing one after another from what was called "summer complaint," Matt's father, thinking he had recognized a trend and that infants were going to keep on dying at that rate, had gone out and bought one hundred baby coffins from a dealer in Oklahoma City. He'd used up twenty-six that first summer and fall, but after that the mysterious disease never struck again, and he was stuck with the rest of them, except for an occasional stillbirth or crib death. The past week the Carltons' baby had been born with an atrophied brain stem and died a few hours later, and when Matt went to take one of the little boxes off the stack to use for the funeral he had found it filled with mice. In fact mice had nested in all of them and spoiled them, so Matt was making a bonfire. Meanwhile, I went downtown to get a haircut so that when I met Sarah at the Passion Play I wouldn't have to hear her complain about how my personal appearance was beginning to degenerate to the same level as my living conditions.

At first the conversation in the barbershop was about the fight that had broken out at the Little Miss Blairsville contest that had been held earlier in the afternoon. This pageant for five-year-olds had been interrupted by a fight between two women, Carla Weston and her ex-husband Don's girlfriend, a girl from Winona named Wanda. Both of the women went down to the front of the stage to take photographs of Carla's and Don's daughter Becky at the same time, and before anyone knew what was happening the two of them were rolling on the ground pulling each other's hair, clawing each other's faces, and kicking each other's shinbones. They were separated, but then when little Becky was chosen as one of the ten semifinalists Carla and Wanda both came forward once more to take more pictures and the fighting started all over again. It was awful. The police had to be called to break it up, the little girl started crying and ran off the stage, and to top things off, after all that trauma the child wasn't even chosen to be one of the top five finalists.

Once this topic was exhausted the conversation reverted to its usual subject. There must be something about the smell of hair tonic, and the feel of the sure hands of the barber on a man's skull, and the soft whirring of the electric clippers, and the stropping of a sharp steel razor on leather, that makes men think about nookie. Oh sometimes the talk is on other subjects. If a railroad man is there it might be about the quicksand they had to try to set rails on, even while the gandy dancers were sinking in up to their hips and the bed couldn't be made solid. Or if a hunter is there it might be about how he was out in the deer woods when fourteen inches of rain fell in seven hours, turning every creek and trickle into a deadly torrent that washed away five men and trapped dozens of others on remote mountainsides for three days until the waters went down. But sooner or later all these tales give way to the subject of copulation. This was especially true in Ames's father's barbershop because in his time Beryl was an even bigger poon hound than Ames. His legendary exploits included being the man who was doing Sally Winter on the edge of a sink in the Grafton Hotel when the sink tore out of the wall and flooded the floor below, and also being the last man to sleep with Amelia Heller—the woman who, because a stroke at the age of twelve had paralyzed one side of her vagina, was said to have the tightest intimate parts in town—before the car she was in was hit head-on by a gravel truck and she was killed.

I wasn't paying much attention to what was being said, just waiting my turn while reading a magazine, until Herbert Selvidge started talking. Herbert was a stutterer and his hands jittered like he had the palsy, though it might just have been the shakes of an old alky. He was being treated for alopecia areata (baldness in spots). His hair had started falling out in tufts and handfuls, leaving bare areas that gradually grew back in, but in a different color than the original strands. Some spots were red, some gray, but his usual hair color was brown. Beryl tried to tell him that it was due to nerves, but Herbert wouldn't have it. "B-b-b-b-but B-b-b-b-beryl," he'd say, "I'm n-n-n-not n-n-n-n-nervous!" Herbert tended to make his declarations short because he knew how brief the attention span of most listeners is for someone afflicted the way he was. He was also hard-of-hearing, and so he usually interrupted when someone else was talking. That day, right in the middle of

Norton Wheeler's shave (a difficult operation because Norton had whiskers everywhere except on his tongue and his eyeballs), just as Beryl was telling about the time he wore the knees out of his pants frigging Maisy Butcher on the hardwood floor of her dining room while her husband was in the garage trying to spray away the fur and blood from a raccoon he'd smashed into on the highway with the grill of his Oldsmobile, Herbert blurted out "I heard W-w-w-wayne S-s-s-slavings's w-w-w-wife is f-f-f-fucking around ag-g-g-g-gain!" This announcement sent a burning sensation up the back of my neck. By the time Herbert got to the end of his sentence I had already had plenty of time to fully experience the brain-paralyzing anxiety his beginning words had provoked. The walls of the room, with its stuffed delirious beasts grinning their shit-eating grins frozen in the rictus of violent death and formaldehyde marination, began to reel around me. Of course I couldn't show it outwardly, I had to sit there calmly and laugh and leer and make snarking noises with the rest of the losers, but as I did so I couldn't help thinking that if the word was making the rounds in the barbershop, while sideburns were being lathered and nosehairs clipped, it must also be circulating in the beauty parlor, where the town gossips congregated and toasted their newly laquered hair-dos underneath the beehive hairdryers. And if the news was loose in the beauty parlor it must also already be percolating around and over the slick green and white formica of the drugstore coffeeshop counter. And from the slurped chocolate malteds and smeared grilled cheese sandwiches of the drugstore countertop it was just a short hop, skip, and a jump to the polluted fog of the pool hall and the awful and bloody world of Wayne Slavings's vengeance.

I didn't know what to do. I was in a state of near shell-shock. The back of my neck was red-hot and my head felt as light as a helium balloon. As soon as I could walk out without attracting too much attention, I left the barbershop, without getting a haircut. I started walking down the street but I didn't know where to go, so

I turned behind the Oddfellows Hall and stood there and tried to think, a process that was complicated by the fact that all during the afternoon Matt and I had sampled both our own product and the products of others, and I had a pretty good buzz going. Through this buzzing several distinct options for action presented themselves to me in quick succession. The first and not very realistic one was to run home, like a child, to my father, tell him everything and leave it up to him to devise a plan to save my skin. In spite of everything that had happened, that still seemed to offer the greatest shelter from harm. But when I imagined having to explain to my father exactly what kind of trouble I was in and how I had gotten into it, I dropped the idea completely, since it seemed likely to send him into an even greater paroxysm of disgust than any of my previous peccadilloes. Dad, notwithstanding that he was planking Lettie Gillis, had a very Old Testament view of morality, at least insofar as it applied to anyone other than himself. And though he wasn't as conversant with Biblical punishments as Mrs. Tollner, who had read the Bible completely through every year for the past seventeen consecutive years, and knew that the word *and* appears in it 46,227 times and that the book of Esther is the only book in the Bible in which the word *God* doesn't appear and that Deuteronomy 22:22 specifies that "if a man be found lying with a woman married to a husband, then they shall both of them die, both the man that lay with the woman, and the woman," I had serious doubts that he would have much sympathy for my current predicament. (Had my father been a diligent Bible reader he certainly would have been interested in some of the other stipulations found in the book of Deuteronomy, such as that of Chapter 23, Verses 12–13 regarding the rules of sanitation to be followed by the soldiers of Israel: "Thou shalt have a place also without the camp, whither thou shalt go forth abroad: And thou shalt have a paddle upon they weapon; and it shall be, when thou wilt ease thyself abroad, thou shalt dig therewith, and shalt turn back and cover that which cometh from thee.")

The second option involved rushing over to the funeral home to find Matt and have him drive me to Corder, where I could catch the seven o'clock bus to St. Louis, and from there to Timbuktu and points east. This idea had a certain pleasing quality to it. I could see myself on the Great Southern Coach passing first through the flat farmlands, then rising up into the hills around Appleton and Bell Junction, crossing the river at Meadeville where the bus usually stopped to pick up that day's batch of released convicts (on one bus trip I'd heard some outstanding harmonica playing by a musician/manslaughterer who'd served eleven years for killing somebody and while in prison had played every year in the orchestra at the Governor's New Year's Eve Ball) and then roaring on up through Mounds, Dongola and Anna—the location of the nuthouse where they took Stanley Hitchins for a spell. When he got out he came back to Blairsville and ran for the school board on the grounds he had a certificate verifying that he was sane, and could his opponent say as much? (He won.) After St. Louis the vision of this journey became a little fuzzy because I hadn't been any further than that, but to my mind this plan had much to recommend it, chiefly getting as far away from potential danger as possible, as opposed to hanging around and finding myself being strung upside down from a tree branch and left to bleed to death like a slaughtered hog.

But before I'd gone half a block in the direction of the funeral home I stopped, because I started imagining what Matt would say. I was sure he'd say that I was panicking. That I was overreacting. That Wayne Slavings was three hundred miles away on a tugboat on the Mississippi River, making sure twelve barges loaded with Peabody Coal Company coal made it past all the snags and sandbars and eddies and arrived safely at the Vicksburg docks. That we still had five gallons of Woodenhead's brew on order to sell that night and if I was ridiculous enough to be pissing in my pants because a *deaf* man said he *heard* something, I should at least stay and help him dispose of the liquor and settle up with Woodenhead on Sunday. Then if I continued to insist on slinking out of town with my tail between my legs I could easily depart on Monday morning, which would still be four days before Wayne was even due back from the river. This hybrid voice, which wasn't completely Matt's voice or even my voice, but most likely some internal voice generated by guilt and the desire to be punished—even I knew it was a lousy thing to do to be screwing another man's wife while he was off earning a living—convinced me to consider a third option, which was to find Rachel and ask her if she knew what was going on, hoping against hope that even if it was known that Rachel was fucking around, perhaps it still wasn't known who it was she was fucking around with. Who knows, I might be in the clear, and not having to be running around like a chicken with its head cut off, hysterically visualizing my own imminent dismemberment. I liked this idea a lot, so much so that only briefly did I even entertain the notion that if Rachel were under suspicion it might not be such a wise thing to be seen talking to her in public. It didn't really matter, because in the end I was too filled with anxiety and dread *not* to go see her. I couldn't endure the eight more hours of uncertainty that remained until the rendezvous she and I had arranged for later on that night. So, with the sensation of a thousand trapped starlings flapping their wings wildly against the inner walls of my skull, I set out to look for her.

I knew where to find her. As the daughter of a veteran, she was working at the American Legion booth at the fairgrounds, selling raffle tickets for such prizes as ice chests, shotguns, quilts, and ten frozen turkeys. In previous years the Legion had tried releasing live turkeys above the crowd so that whoever could catch one got to keep it. But the first year when they set them loose from the roof of City Hall the turkeys wisely used their wings to sail a quarter of a mile outside of town and escaped into the woods, and the second year when they tried clipping the turkeys' wings before they launched them this backfired, too, because it was like dropping twenty-pound turkey bombs onto the packed crowd waiting down below, and there were several injuries suffered by people hit in the head and face by the panicked birds. With the frozen ones, everybody went home happy.

I got to the fairgrounds, but I didn't find Rachel right away, because of the universal law that decrees that whenever you desperately need to find one particular person, you always run into other people you aren't looking for and don't want to see. These kind of nuisance encounters were especially likely to happen on Homecoming Weekend, because a lot of people came back home to visit then who weren't around most of the rest of the year. As luck would have it the first person I ran into at the fairgrounds was Dawson Fitts, a distant relation of mine who had moved out of the county a couple of years before and who no one in the family missed one bit because no one liked Dawson, not even his own parents. When he was little I'd watched in awe as his mother had chased him across the yard with a tree limb, whopping him in the hind end until Dawson crawled into the doghouse to get away from her. Even then she didn't stop but stood there poking that limb in at him like he was some kind of an animal, shouting, "Come out of there right now you little shit!" Never before or after had I heard anyone's mother call them a "little shit," so this event had stuck in my memory. Dawson was there in the livestock-showing area, appraising the stock, looking at buying a bull to service his heifers, but since he was notoriously tightfisted—people used to say he was so cheap he wouldn't pay a nickel to see a piss-ant eat a bale of hay—he wasn't having much luck. As soon as he saw me he latched onto my arm, gave me a bear hug like I was his long-lost dear cousin and best friend, and slobbered all over my shirt.

He was drunk and sentimental and kept asking me if I remembered the time he'd broken the nose of a carpenter who had tried to cheat him on the price of some green lumber. I told him I didn't remember and that I was in a hurry and after promising him I'd catch up with him later on to do some drinking together I managed to escape. I'd barely freed myself from Dawson's grasp when I ran into another cattleman, Gig Boyd, a golfing buddy of my father's. Gig was a terrible slicer. He tried to compensate for it by lining his feet up at a forty-five degree angle to the left, and it actually worked. It looked funny as hell, though. His ball would start out way off over the left rough then curve back like a boomerang to the right and wind up in the middle of the fairway. He was about a sixteen handicap. Gig was drunk and babbling, too. He took my arm and insisted on telling me how he'd lost a calf and its mother the previous week. The mother was trying to give birth, but the calf was stuck, so he'd had to pull the calf out with a chain and a winch. By the time he finally got the calf out it was already dead, and in the process the cow had pulled tendons in her back legs, so that afterward she could only get up on her front legs. From lying down so much she got sores on her stomach, the green flies went to working on her and she got fly-blown. "The maggots were eating her alive," he said. "Then her kidneys locked. When we cut her open she was all corrupt up under her bladder. The vet said if she didn't have a fever, make hamburger out of her. Shit, I wouldn't eat any of that meat, would you? Would you eat that meat?" I assured him that no indeed, I wouldn't eat hamburger from a fly-blown cow, even an unfevered one, and continued trying just to get away from him, but he kept saying "Hell no, you wouldn't eat that," and told me what he'd done with the cow, how he'd shot it and fed part of it to his dogs and put the rest out for the crows to pick clean. Gig, like most people, was aware of the feud between me and my father, and as I was backing away trying to get out of earshot he was still braying at me: "Ray, don't forget your family!

Family is everything!" I didn't bother to point out that he was just as much in need of this advice as I was, considering the fight he'd had with his sister over their inheritance. He got so mad at her he had his house jacked up, put on beams, and turned around to face the opposite direction so he wouldn't have to look out his living room window and see her home across the street.

Gig's voice was still audible behind me as I turned the corner leading to the midway. Next to the entrance to the sideshow featuring the Two-Headed Baby I got a bit of a jolt at the sight of our former chicken farmer, Donk, standing in front of the exhibit. Donk didn't see me. He was jingling dimes and nickels in the palm of his hand and was engaged in a state of deep communion with the advertisement for the attraction, a rather crude hand-painted poster of a double-headed infant. He seemed to be trying to decide whether it was worth paying fifteen cents to see something here at the carnival that he could probably see at home for free. I would have liked to have seen the two-headed baby myself, but I didn't want to get stuck in any more conversations, even one with Donk, which was bound to be fraught with great import and valuable information about the meaning of the recent heavy flights of brown moths—whether they portended an early fall, or a late winter, or just a lot of yellow splats on car windshields. So I kept on walking past the freak show arcade, around the corner of the Chamber of Commerce booth, where the frymasters were serving up deep-fried Willow River suckerfish, and entered that part of the midway where I knew Rachel would be ensconced distributing raffle tickets. That's when I found myself with an excellent view, in profile, from a distance of about forty yards, of the terrible visage of Wayne Slavings.

Wayne was standing outside the booth talking to Rachel, and neither one of them looked very happy. Wayne wasn't happy, I would later learn, because he'd gotten word from his buddy Cletus Hicks that while setting illegal trotlines up at Eleven Mile

Slough, Cletus had seen Rachel riding in a car with another man, and so Wayne had taken unauthorized shore leave to come home and find out the truth of the matter. This was the first time I'd seen the two of them together, because the previous times Wayne had come home I had taken care to stay out of their way. And though they didn't seem to be particularly joyful at that particular moment—which surprisingly, given Wayne's reputation, wasn't one of harsh language or blows but consisted, at least the part I saw, of Wayne with his hands on his hips staring down at the ground in an angry yet injured pose, waiting for an answer, and Rachel talking to him in what seemed to be a semi-defiant manner as she faced down his accusations—they did seem to belong together in a much more profound way than I had ever imagined myself being with anyone, either with Rachel or even with Sarah for that matter. In that moment I began to understand the nature of my trespass against Wayne, and one part of me felt that he would be perfectly justified in whaling the tar out of me.

There was plenty of time to turn and run before he saw me and maybe escape unscathed, but the kind of stunned fear that causes the guinea pig to freeze in front of the anaconda at feeding time at the zoo kept me glued to the spot, until my fear began to act like a magnet and Wayne's head began to swivel, almost in slow motion, in my direction. His head stopped swiveling when his eyes locked onto mine, and in that moment we silently cemented our connection as victim and avenger: he knew, I knew he knew, and he knew I knew he knew. In the next split second I had just enough time to glance quickly at Rachel and see her jaw dropped open in an expression that I read as one of disbelief that I had been idiot enough to intrude upon this situation she was in the process of talking her way out of (she was infinitely quicker mentally than Wayne and, except for the slipup over the Alvin Bowers incident, usually managed to keep him in the dark about her activities) before I looked back at Wayne and our eyes locked again. It was as his stare took on a hard look full of malice and hatred that I began to feel intensely that life was a good thing, that an intact body was something to be cherished and preserved, and that a head without skull fractures or knife lacerations was clearly preferable to one that was battered and bleeding. I remembered the way Harvey Weems's face had looked that morning at the funeral home when Matt and I had slipped inside to filch the embalming fluid. Harvey's body was lying on the slab with fishing line coming out of his mouth because Matt's father was trying to put a smile on his face. I'm sure Harvey wasn't smiling when he got blown off the dragline and landed on a tree stump fifty feet away, but Matt's father always did his best to give the families of the deceased what they wanted, and what Harvey's wife wanted was a smile on Harvey's face. So Matt's father's had sunk fishhooks into the corners of Harvey's lips and hung weights on the end of the line that ran up over his face and forehead to where it could dangle off the end of the table and draw the muscles upward. Harvey was smiling, but he was dead. I wanted to be able to smile while I was still alive, so I turned and ran for my life.

In my eighteen years of life I'd done a lot of things that deserved punishment. As a twelve-year-old I had demolished the Dillard's mailbox with cherry bombs on at least three different occasions and never been apprehended. While still just a malevolent young child filled with curiosity about the miracle of winged insect flight, I'd clipped the wings of migrating Monarch butterflies with scissors to see if they could still fly on with only half their wingspan left (bad luck on their part to have paused to catch their breath midway through their two-thousand-mile flight in perhaps the only yard in the entire state where this particular kind of mutilation was a regular feature). At the age of thirteen I'd burned down the Jamison's tool shed, and I still don't know how I got fingered for that piece of destruction. Matt and I had built a long fuse out of a bedsheet and some gunpowder and were sitting at home innocently playing Chutes and Ladders at the kitchen table when the thing went up in flames. Yet even as the Fire Department was hosing down the embers the two of us were dragged out of the house and handed over to old man Jamison for three months of servitude doing yard work and washing his car. But up until that summer I'd never done anything that would lead anyone to want to kill me, and now that I had, there seemed to be no alternative left to me except to try my best to keep Wayne from wringing my neck. I'm not a particularly fast runner, and I'd never run for my life before, but as it turns out it doesn't require any special knowledge. You just run as fast as you can and as far as you can and turn corners and cut through yards and duck under clotheslines and scat through hedges and look behind you every chance you get to see if Death is catching up to you. At first I was really only walking for my life, strictly speaking, though at a pretty brisk clip. Those first immediate rapidly performed steps took me behind the men's bathroom, between two parked trucks, under the fence that separated the fairgrounds from the high school football field, over the cable that demarcated the boundary between the football field and the alley, and then into the alley itself. That's where I began my actual running per se, and it wasn't until I was halfway across the playground behind the elementary school that I even looked back for the first time. I didn't see Wayne behind me, but I still didn't slow down. From that point I zigged and zagged through the Gilkey's vegetable garden, sprinted down the path behind the Mulder's garage, cut between the Wakefields' and Hawkinses' houses, dodged the Hodge's chained German shepherd that had once knocked Donna Lummer off her bike and bit her on the ass and ankle, and raced down the alley behind Mr. and Mrs. Worthington's house, the couple who had founded the local library and started the Blairsville Museum collection with the gift of an ostrich egg they'd picked up somewhere on their travels. After that there was a long straight lope down the alley behind the Catholic church where I was protected by hedges on both sides, then more ninety-degree turns to throw off any pursuers, and then, just at the point where I had to stop running or puke, I paused behind the icehouse where Karen Ricker, one of my high school classmates, had gone to work after graduation but only lasted two weeks before quitting because her boss kept asking her to let him put his cold hands inside her blouse to warm them up. I'd covered a good mile and a half by that time.

Naturally when one is running for one's life the thoughts that predominate are primarily those concerned with the short-term survival of the organism: how to avoid being caught and where to go to find safety. But even as I made my serpentine path toward Mrs. Naylor's, where I intended to gather some clothes and my driver's license then hightail it out of town following the railroad tracks, there was time for other thoughts to rise up in my consciousness as well, and some of these thoughts were concerned with what my situation would be when all the dust settled. First, it seemed pretty certain that my affair with Rachel was over, one way or another. That much seemed obvious, and the absoluteness of that fact led me to consider the current state of my relationship with Sarah, whom I had been treating quite shoddily for some time now. I began to chastise myself. What could I have been thinking all this time? How could I have behaved so reprehensibly, and with such callousness, for so long? I was suddenly overwhelmed with remorse, a remorse that I had done my best to squelch completely for the past two months. I was starting to feel sorry not just for my out-and-out philandering, which represented the highest attainable point on the culpability scale, but also for all the petty little things I had done, like not showing up on time, or not showing up at all, when I had promised I would, leaving Sarah to shower me with tears, recriminations, and the occasional body blow the next time I saw her. All at once, after all that time, I felt bad about what I'd done and not done, and when I looked at my watch and saw that it was after six o'clock, I felt yet another sharp pang, because I knew that at that very moment not half a mile away Sarah was waiting for me forlornly at the high school auditorium where we were supposed to watch the Passion Play together. It was enough to enflame my tear ducts, though no actual exudate appeared because during the frenzied crazy-legged flight from the fairgrounds I had already sweated out ninety-nine percent of my currently available body fluids.

I felt like a cad. I was in the wrong and I knew it. It wasn't Sarah's fault she wanted to marry me, and even if it was, she didn't deserve to be punished for it in this manner. With the help of my newly revived conscience, which was aided in no little way by the realization that I no longer had any choice in the matter, at least as far as continuing to see Rachel, there behind the forty-foot tall wall of the icehouse, with its chilled bricks slick with condensation and its constant wispy cloud of water vapor hovering just above the roof, I resolved to turn over a new leaf, for good this time. I wasn't sure I wanted to be married, but I figured if Sarah had her heart set on being engaged, then I could at least grant her that, if only for the time being, as long as it didn't actually bind me to anything definite in the future. Such were my magnanimous thoughts, in the shadow of the icehouse, as I paused in my passage toward destiny.

Meanwhile at the Passion Play, where I imagined (mistakenly as it turned out) Sarah sitting so sadly alone, a number of remarkable occurrences were taking place, not the least of them being the performance of the play itself, which as it unfolded was turning into the most memorable exhibition of Biblical theater the town had ever known. This was because several of the key performers were not only crocked to the gills on moonshine but possibly even poisoned to the point of near-delirium by the toxicity of the "flavorings" the liquor was spiced with that year. One especially vivid appearance was turned in by old Mr. Willholm—a bony leather-skinned weasel of a man with a nose like a hatchet and eyes like a lizard who had been elected city attorney for twenty-two years in a row—who was playing the disciple Peter this year. He was so soused he was totally lost and bewildered during the play, so much so that the second time he was asked by the Roman soldiers— Arthur Kennet and Roger Masterson, both a little shaky themselves in their leggings and shields—if he knew the man Jesus of Nazareth whom they'd just arrested, he got genuinely annoyed at their persistence, and when they questioned him for the third time, as required to do by scripture and the script of the play, he said, "How many times do I have to tell you I don't *know* the son of a b—." He managed to swallow this last word before it spilled out of his mouth, but when he heard the cock crow—Ted Corning playing a sound effects record—to signal daybreak and Peter's third denial of Christ, he remembered what he was doing and slunk away abashed, which actually was perfectly in keeping with Peter's comportment in the Bible, and therefore a most effective piece of theater. But the highlight of the evening—or lowlight depending on your point of view—was the performance of Herb Hillman, who had played Jesus for thirteen years and who many of the younger Sunday School children had come to believe was actually Jesus himself. Well this year Jesus was drunk. Herb was totally inebriated on stage, a circumstance that in some people's opinion (an extreme minority, to be sure) added an element of verve to his acting that had been missing for far too long. Allen Price declared Herb's uninhibited performance to be the best of his entire career, at least in the beginning, when he was healing lepers left and right and casting out demons with great authority. But things started getting problematical as the play went on, and the real trouble started when Mary Magdalene, played by Herb's wife, Nell, started drying his feet with her hair and Herb began to giggle. He tried to stifle it, but it was too much for him. The accompanist pounded wildly on the piano keys to cover it up, but Herb could still be heard laughing. Nell turned red and tried to glare at him to calm him down, but it took a sharp twist on his ankle to finally get his attention. Everyone could see her hissing at him to straighten up and behave, and the first ten rows plainly heard Herb reply, "Damn it, I can't help it, it tickles!" Things went downhill from there. On the way to his crucifixion Herb dropped the cross clean off the stage and onto the floor, where the papier-mâché and chicken wire construction fell to pieces. Herb peered over the edge of the stage at it as if he expected it to magically rise back up into his arms, and when it didn't he turned to the audience and said, "Ah, the hell with it," and continued his trek without it. This pretty well ruined the impact of the crucifixion scene because they had to use a hastily hammered-together cross held up by two men standing beside it that wouldn't have fooled a three-year-old. Then, in the scene at the tomb Herb—who was supposed to use the time between the scene where he was placed in the tomb and the scene where the stone is rolled away from the entrance to sneak out the tomb's back exit and into the wings—apparently passed out inside and failed to slip out in time. So at the moment when the women arrived to anoint the body, with the tomb opened and an angel (Floyd Spees) guarding the cave, instead of finding Jesus gone and resurrected they found Herb inside the tomb stone drunk, crawling around on his death bier. This was the last straw for many people. Many of them stood up and left angry, and for a long time afterward Matt and I, as representatives of the moonshine sellers, got the blame for having caused an entire generation of young people to veer dissolutely toward atheism.

Back at the icehouse, I had more pressing problems to deal with than a bunch of eight-year-olds' crises of faith. I was feeling better, better ethically, because I felt myself less of a moral degenerate after the resurgence of my affection for Sarah, and better physically from the opportunity to get a second wind and being able to breathe without the danger of gagging on my own tongue. Still, when I started moving again I was moving much more slowly, painfully slowly, not running now but walking, desperately casting my eyes in all directions, daring to imagine that I might actually be home free, since there was absolutely no sign that my pursuers had managed to follow my meandering trail, but suffering immensely because I had an incredibly piercing cramp in my left side that kept stabbing into my lungs. Thankfully, Mrs. Naylor's boardinghouse, repository of freedom, loomed just a half block ahead of me. On the front porch I could see Tony at his usual station, peering through the screen, hands out of sight, almost certainly busy playing with himself. Tony had been in a very agitated state lately, to the point that he had even taken to roaming the hall stark naked at times. All the activity in town recently had unhinged him. He had come to believe that the preparations for the Homecoming Festival had something to do with him. He'd heard about a collection for a charity drive and in his mind this got translated into a conspiracy being conducted by local businessmen who had banded together to collect money to be used against him in some way. A few days before he'd shown me a letter he'd written and was going to send to the mayor to exonerate himself of charges he was sure were about to be brought against him. I had tried to explain to Tony that this was probably the annual Charity Fund collection and had nothing to do with him, but he said the radio station was in on it, too, and had been transmitting radio waves that attacked his sexual organs and made him behave badly. He said he was working on an electrical device that would counter these attacks by neutralizing the radio waves, and he was sure that once the Chamber of Commerce realized they couldn't get him by means of radio signals, they would try other means to send him back to the institution, so he was preparing all manner of defenses against the coming onslaught.

As I approached closer to the front door of the boardinghouse

I heard an ambulance siren wailing in the distance, but I didn't think anything of it. I was too busy plotting my next move, which would be to get safely to Walking Tom's shack on Cypress Creek, where I could hole up until I could get word to Matt to come and get me. Walking Tom was one of a group of middle-aged men who congregated on the street corners downtown and spent their afternoons and evenings drinking and socializing. Some of them were slightly off in the head, like Willis Dearborn, who would sit on a cushion he brought with him and make barking noises at the passing cars. Another one was Olaf Merrick, who rumor had it, was actually a rich man with stocks and bonds and jewelry socked away in a safe deposit box. But rich or poor, what he preferred to do with his time was hang out downtown with his comrades, enjoying his daily whiskey. Lately, due to Woodenhead's fear of attracting unwanted attention from the authorities, Woodenhead had decided he didn't want us driving up to his house anymore to make our pickups, and he had started using Walking Tom's place as a drop-off point for the liquor. He would put the jugs in gunnysacks and give them to Walking Tom, who would then hide them beneath the water's surface by tying the bags to tree roots with rope. Walking Tom was strange, but completely trustworthy and independent to the degree that, not wanting to be beholden to other people, he walked the two miles to town and back every day and never accepted a ride from anyone, not even Woodenhead. His house had no running water, and he bathed, when he bathed, in the creek. It was such an out-of-the-way location that no one would think to look for me there, and that would be a good thing.

I went in the front door of the boardinghouse. Tony had already vanished up the stairway ahead of me. The rest of the place was quiet. I climbed the stairs and went into my room, where I hurriedly grabbed my belongings and stuffed them into a pillowcase. (My suitcase was unavailable because it was in the garage at the funeral home filled with empty pint bottles we had to return to Woodenhead that night). The fact was not lost on me that this was the second time in two months I had been ousted from my home under duress and with virtually no notice. It was more than a little bit annoying to be driven from pillar to post in such a manner, and I silently pledged to myself that in the future I would do my very best to insure that when I left a place I'd been living it would be on my own terms and following a schedule of my own creation. With the pillowcase in my hand and my wallet in my pocket (I left ten dollars for the week's overdue rent on the dresser with a note for Mrs. Naylor) I softly slipped into the hallway and shut the door behind me.

I was walking down the hall toward the stairs when I suddenly heard an ear-splitting screech of tires in front of the boardinghouse. I ran to the hall window to look out to see what it was, and of course it was Wayne. He wasn't alone either. With him were two of his fellow white trash goons. These three messengers of doom all jumped out of a wretched-looking GMC pickup with no front grill and half a windshield and ran directly toward the front door. Within seconds I could hear the sound of heavy boots galumphing up the stairs. I had to think fast. I didn't want to go back to my room, because that's where they would come looking first and I didn't want to be trapped there. The fire escape from the third floor to the back alley was outside a window in Mrs. Tollner's room, so that was the way to safety. I ran down the hall and twisted the doorknob (I didn't knock, because I didn't want the sound to be heard below), opened the door and walked right in, interrupting Mrs. Tollner and Imogene's evening prayer service. The two ladies were in their room and not at the Passion Play because they belonged to a splinter denomination of Pentecostals called the "Tabernacle Voice of God Through Christ the Savior on Calvary," which disapproved of the presentation of such dramas. This congregation had a number of curious beliefs. For one thing they attributed all the troubles in the world today to the fact that the

Lost Day, lost when the sun stopped over the valley of Gibeon to allow Joshua to complete his conquest of the Philistines, had never been recovered, and until it was there would be nothing but woe and misery down here on earth. While waiting for Jesus to come back to sort things out there was nothing to do but baptize every living wavering soul in His name to assure their salvation, so the Voice of Godders had conducted their own revival this past week, dunking people like crazy. On Friday alone twenty-seven were immersed in the brown silty waters of the Willow River, an event that had repercussions in Grandpa's house, because Grandpa's cook, Nola, left work early to attend it and therefore hadn't had time to cook him a hot lunch but had left a cold plate in the refrigerator. When he scolded her for this dereliction of duty she said she couldn't help it, that she had to do the Lord's work. "Then let the Lord pay your goddamn salary!" was Grandpa's reply.

The moment I burst into the Tollner's room both Mrs. Tollner and Imogene started screaming, partly because they were frightened out of their wits and partly because they hated to be seen without their makeup on. They started frantically scurrying around, Mrs. Tollner to try to fit a wig on her head and Imogene to rub the cold cream off her face. Without slowing down I shouted out what I hoped sounded like a sincere though brief apology, and I ran right across the room to the window, which, I discovered too late and only after wrestling in vain with the sash, was nailed shut. By then Wayne and his thugs, who had located the source of the disturbance that was now rousing the entire population of the boardinghouse, came barging in the room like stampeding buffalo, and I was forced to turn and face my pursuers.

The battle was joined in a matter of seconds. I got a few moments' respite when Petey dive-bombed the intruders' faces, pecking and striking with his beak and flapping his wings in their eyes, but that only lasted until Wayne's buddy Cletus grabbed a towel off a hook on the door and, wielding it like a whip, popped Petey in mid-air, plucking him right out of the sky. He fell to the floor with a thud, and for all intents and purposes appeared to have been dispatched to the great birdfeeder in the sky. This sight caused Imogene, who before a herniated disk and asthma attacks debilitated her had had no trouble lifting two hundred pound shut-ins from hospital bed to gurney and back, to start walloping the gang of rogues with her ironing board while yelling, "We'll sue! We'll sue!" a resounding and pain-filled wail that penetrated the slumber of Mr. Leclerc down the hall. This worthy, hearing what to him seemed to be cries of "Sioux! Sioux!", was immediately catapulted back into the nineteenth-century Indian Wars and, grabbing his grandfather's saber off the wall, came roaring down the corridor and into the room in a belated and hallucinatory attempt to try to save his spread-eagled ancestor from the grisly fate that awaited him. But Mr. Leclerc was no match for Wayne's cousin Corliss, who effortlessly deprived him of his cutlass, turned him around and shoved him back into the hall, slamming the door behind him.

The upshot of all this turmoil was that I quickly found myself backed into a corner alone, directly facing the brutish and sadistic features of a half-crazed and cuckolded Wayne, the only thing standing between me and utter destruction being Dad's pistol, which, happily, I discovered myself to be holding tightly gripped in my right hand. While packing to leave I had thrown it into the pillowcase with my clothes, not really thinking I would actually ever need to use it, but feeling more comfortable just knowing it was around. And now, with no conscious memory of having reached into the pillowcase and dug it out of its cloth wrappings, there I was aiming the end of the barrel at a point just above the spot where Wayne's bushy Neanderthal eyebrows joined together. At the sound of the cocking of the hammer, Wayne stopped where he was, about six feet away from me.

The next moment probably lasted only a few seconds, but it seemed like an extraordinarily long time to me. I watched Wayne eye the gun, giving every appearance that he was doing some thinking. I was hoping one of his thoughts was that it might be a good idea for him to walk out of the room, leave the building, and not come back, but I didn't really expect things to be that easy. I was doing some thinking, too. I knew I didn't want to have to shoot Wayne. I knew I wanted the sight of the barrel staring right into his face to be enough of a deterrent to convince him that this was a situation he would do well to extricate himself from. Unfortunately, that was not the case. After those initial seconds of hesitation the presence of the gun only seemed to act as a further incentive to Wayne to proceed with his intentions, as though now it really made things worthwhile. At some point the thought probably even occurred to him that in fact it was a lucky thing for him that I did have a gun, because it saved him the trouble of having to go home and retrieve his own hogleg .44. Instead, all he would have to do was take this one away from me and then use it himself.

Whatever his train of thought, the time for thinking was over. Wayne was ready to act, and he began slowly advancing on me, one small step at a time. I warned him that I was about to shoot, but he just grinned his snaggle-tooth grin and held his two-thumbed hand up like he was pulling the trigger himself, firing right into my face. I guess it was that gesture of cockiness on his part that gave me the impetus to decide to fire. Even though I was the guilty party in this matter, there was no need to rub my face in it by ignoring me and my gun so humiliatingly. I pulled the trigger.

It's probably just as well that what happened next happened, because I really didn't want to be a murderer, and I didn't play an instrument, so it was likely that my time in prison wouldn't be as enjoyably spent as the fellow I met on the bus who at least got to go outside the prison walls one night a year and play music for the governor. As I pulled back on the trigger I felt something fall and bounce off my wrist, and this was immediately followed by the noise of pieces of metal hitting the floor. I looked down and saw that the hammer had fallen right out, clean off, followed by the cylinder, and the bullets had bounced out of it and were now rolling harmlessly across the slanted hardwood underneath Mrs. Tollner's bed. In this split second of time, as I considered the undeniable empirical fact that my gun had disintegrated in my hand, my thoughts were carried back to the day two weeks before when Mr. Leclerc, with whom I had become friendly as a result of spending many mornings together while he ate his cereal and juice and stool softeners, had offered to clean the weapon for me. The metal had become corroded and encrusted with crud because when I'd first moved into the boardinghouse I'd stashed the gun in an unused chimney flue, a location that had turned out to be a prime collecting tank for rainwater. Now it was apparent that in spite of his years in the army and his seemingly knowledgeable use of jeweler's rouge and three-in-one oil, Mr. Leclerc, when reassembling the gun, had neglected to replace some piece that was vital to its operating mechanisms. Later on it occurred to me that I should have known better than to entrust such a task to a man who, for all his tales of martial heroics, had not been an actual bearer and user of arms himself but had functioned chiefly as a quartermaster or supply flunky for most of his military career. The adventures with which he regaled me between spoonfuls of bran flakes were not his own, but those of his crucified grandfather and his larger-than-life great-grandfather, one Baptiste Leclerc, who had been one of the earliest settlers of this part of the country and had been involved in countless skirmishes with the original inhabitants. The most famous of his exploits was an encounter known as the Battle of Carney Creek, where Baptiste, holed up in a log cabin in the small settlement of Creve Coeur with his wife, his wife's sister and her husband, and a third man, who ultimately proved useless during the ensuing siege because he was so terrified he hid in a corner and spent the entire duration of the battle reciting his rosary, came under attack by a large war party of Indians. With the two women casting balls and cutting patches so that Baptiste and his brother-in-law could keep firing, they killed fourteen Indians and wounded many more in the first half hour of the battle. But instead of being discouraged by this high casualty rate the attackers became even more determined to prevail. Realizing that a direct frontal assault was not going to succeed, the Indians changed their tactics to fastening combustible matter to their arrows and shooting volley after volley of blazing missiles onto the cabin's roof. At first, as each blaze flared up it was put out by the women who threw what little water they had with them onto the burning shingles. But as the fiery arrows showered upon the house without letup, the little band saw that their stock of water would soon dwindle to nothing. Even though the house was near a creek, it would have been suicidal to attempt to run there, fill a bucket, and run back, so they kept applying the water they had until they had used every last drop. When the Indians let loose with yet another volley, the defenders, having no means to extinguish the blazing roof, were forced to contemplate what would be their probable fates: butchery for the men, violation and slavery for the women. Despair began to settle on their spirits. Then, miraculously, one of the females produced a gallon of milk from her breasts. It was immediately poured onto the flames, and when this success was followed by silence on the part of the assailants, it seemed at last as if the attack was being broken off. But suddenly there came another discharge of flaming missiles, this time accompanied by blood-curdling screams arising from a hundred wild throats. Even Baptiste Leclerc himself, whose chiseled face had been the very mirror of a hero's soul, looked aghast at his companions. But at this juncture the noble Baptiste's wife, with an angelic smile on her face, handed her husband a urinal filled with the fluid that would prove the salvation of the garrison. The fire was again put out, and the elastic spirits of the little party sent forth one shout of joy and another of defiance, hurled with spirit in the face of the attackers' exultation. Three times the women supplied from the same fountain a fluid for the extinguishing of the threatening flames, until at last the baffled Indians ran off, screaming a bitter howl of mingled resentment and despair. The courage and steadfastness of Baptiste and his companions didn't go unnoticed. When their achievement was recounted after the battle, some of the young gentlemen in St. Louis united in paying the expense of a fine Cramer rifle to present to M. Baptiste Leclerc, for his gallantry in the defense of the little settlement. But during the time employed in manufacturing the rifle, in some of the conversations that the battle inspired, it was playfully suggested that the ladies also deserved a present for the spirited share they had taken in the conflict, and some thoughtless young man remarked that a silver urinal should be presented to Madame Leclerc. This unfortunate comment was reported to her husband. When the committee arrived at Monsieur Leclerc's abode to present him with the expensive gift as a token of their gratitude, he received them with dignity, examined the firearm carefully, and then stated his opinion in the following manner: "Gentlemen, it is a fuzee of beautiful proportion, containing very much gold in the pan, and silver on his breeches; he is a very gentleman gun for kill de game. I tank you. I shall not take him. Some gentleman have consider to give ma cherie amie one urinal silvare! I tell you sare, I take care of dem tings myself. Go to hell avec votre dam long gun! I shall not take him! Go to hell, any body, by damn sight!!!"

I don't think it mattered ultimately that Mr. Leclerc was insufficiently schooled in gun repair or too old and nearsighted to see that what he was doing was going to make my firearm fall to pieces, because I really don't believe Wayne was going to let anything as inconsequential as a loaded pistol keep him from expressing his dismay and hurt feelings in a physical manner, which is what he now proceeded to do. Mercifully, I only felt the first fifteen or twenty punches, and after that either my head was numb or the shock of the pummeling caused all the blood in my body to rush to my internal organs, so that the rest of the blows he was raining down on me just felt like heavy weights. I felt the pressure, but not the pain. I remember curling up in a ball and I remember having various thoughts like, "So this is what fighting is like" and "So this is what getting the shit beat out of you is like," because in truth I had never been in a fight in my life or even hit anyone unless you count the time I opened the bathroom door at the pool hall and accidentally flattened Randall Giddings's face. I couldn't see anything of what was going on. I had a vague idea that Mrs. Tollner was trying to beat Wayne on the back of his head with her Bible, and that Imogene was hitting him with her iron (the ironing board had gotten shattered in the beginning of the melee), but Wayne wasn't stopping. He was like a fury battering me. At one point I found myself being flung across the room against a radiator, a collison that I felt because the iron bars dug into my back, perhaps the penultimate region to be pounded into insensibility. It was as I lay there stunned at the foot of the radiator, arms and legs splayed out at curious angles, my face turned toward Wayne, that I became aware that a big boot was descending through the air in the general direction of my head. Then came a terrific jolt, and I felt a peculiar floating sensation. Bright blue lights seemed to be going off in the room, so bright that they blinded me. There was an acrid smell like that of a burning electrical cord, and then everything got very quiet. The next thing I knew I opened my eyes for a moment and saw my brother Frank kneeling over me. "What are you doing here?" I said. "Dad had a heart attack," he said. "Thank God," I said, and I passed out.

I dreamed I was gigging frogs. I had a twenty-five-pound lard can with a lantern inside so I could see the frogs' eyes but they couldn't see me. I was ready to gig a big bullfrog but suddenly I had a pain in my back and Donk of all people was standing beside me. I said, "My back hurts." He said, "Stop beating your meat so much. That's what's causing it." Then I was crawling under a house trying to find a leak in some pipes. There was something in front of me and I crawled over it. I could see it was a dead German shepherd, all bloated and foul smelling. I had to throw up. I tried to crawl toward the opening in the foundation where there was light, but I didn't make it, I threw up where I was. Then I was outside and Donk was there again saying, "If your nose itches it's a sign you have company coming hungry. If your right hand itches you're gonna shake hands with a friend, and if your left hand itches it's a sign someone's gonna give you money. There's lots of ways to choke a dog without choking him on butter." Then there was dark, then light, then dark, then light again and I woke up.

It was a day and a half later. I was at home, in my room, staring at a snakeskin on the wall. When my eyes focused I saw the goldfish bowl, my bullwhip, all my belongings. I looked in the mirror, where I discovered that my face was swollen up to where it looked like a rotten canteloupe. I yelled for someone to come, and no one came, and I fell back asleep again.

The next time I woke up Frank was there, and he told me what had happened. On the green of number four at the country club, where Dad had just two-putted to score his second straight par on the first day in a month when his feet felt good enough to enable him to play golf, he had started feeling a pain in his left shoulder. At first he'd tried to shake it off, thinking it was the bursitis that recurred there (as if he didn't have enough aches and pains in his rear and his feet, lately his shoulder had been bothering him) but then it got sharper, and he doubled over and his breath got short and soon it was apparent to his partners that he was in distress, and in half an hour he was in the throes of a full-fledged heart attack. He'd had chest pains before, and was on medication, and had to pee on a piece of colored paper every morning to find out whether his something-or-other count was too high, but this was something new, this was the big hand of God gripping his heart in its fist and squeezing it like it was a pulped grapefruit. The ambulance was called, he was put in it, and just like that he was kidnapped from a leisurely golfing outing on a beautiful afternoon and was on his way to the emergency room of Remser County Hospital seventeen miles away. Frank had got Babe and Mrs. Mims and my mother and had swung around by Mrs. Naylor's to get me and found me getting beaten to death. Everybody's pitched in to grab hold of Wayne but it wasn't until Tony attached an electrode to his back and let him have twelve volts of current from the battery-powered stunning device he'd constructed to use against the businessmen he thought were plotting against him that Wayne let go of me, and even then it took Imogene injecting the how many ever cc's of sodium pentothal into Wayne's veins necessary to knock him out completely before he stopped trying to get to me. That's how my life was saved.

For Dad, the reprieve was more temporary. After a week in the hospital they let him go home, but now his previous troubles seemed like nothing compared to what was in store for him. His body went into open revolt and mutiny, primarily his circulatory system and his pancreas, which decided to stop manufacturing enough insulin. Diabetes set in, and soon various parts of his physique began to abandon him, like rats fleeing a sinking ship. First to go were the traitorous toes of his left foot, which turned purple, green, and luminous black in succession and gave off a highly putrefactive odor. Having relied heavily upon them since birth, naturally he was bitter at this betrayal and agreed to cast them off only with the greatest reluctance and under the direct threat of losing the entire foot and leg. For a time there was no end of excoriating and calumniating of the toes, the doctors who removed them, and a God who would allow such a thing to occur. Dad swore righteous oaths that he would rather die than ever again submit to such a travesty. But the desertion of his toes turned out to be just the first of many such losses. When the gangrene crept into his foot Dad was forced to reconsider his position, which after all he had taken during a period of extreme postoperative stress. In truth, he had little choice. Once again he yielded to the hacksaws and blades of the Hippocratic meat cutters, and by the time they were done with him his left leg had been pruned back all the way to the hip joint, and the right leg followed a year later.

Amputation didn't improve Dad's disposition. It just gave him one more thing to be mad at. There was some benefit in it for me, in that he could no longer haul off and kick me in the behind when the mood struck him. But I paid for it in other ways. Now whenever I was home I had to accompany him on his weekly Sunday pilgrimage to the cemetery to put flowers on his mother's grave. Someone had to hoist him out of the car and into the wheelchair for the trip across the spongy ground to Grandmother's final resting place. It meant nothing to me, Grandmother's grave. The only enduring memory I had kept of her was the time she threw out all the stuffed animals I slept with. "You're too old to sleep with varmints!" she said. (I never forgave her and neither did Billy, Goldie, or Nahum, the three bears who constituted the ruling council of elders among the twenty-odd cloth beasts I bedded down with nightly. Rescued from the trash heap they plotted her death beneath the covers. It would be overstepping the bounds of reason to suppose they had anything to do with it, but it is certainly a fact that she did not long outlive her rash deed.) Not only did I have to wheel Dad to the grave site, I had to manicure it. Weeds had to be pulled up because somewhere in Dad's dark universe dandelions were a defilement to his mother's memory. And forget about cacti. That inoffensive succulent didn't have the right to exist within five feet of Grandmother's blessed mound, never mind that every other grave in the boneyard was quilted with them. No, Grandmother's shrine must be kept pristine. Last week's wilted flowers had to be gathered and put in a paper sack for disposal at home, and fresh ones placed before the tombstone. And not just plopped down in a haphazard fashion either. The exact arrangements dwelling in Dad's funereal imagination had to be duplicated. It always took a good five minutes of fussing with the blossoms before he was satisfied, even if it was zero degrees and my bare hands too numb to function. I had my doubts whether he had gone to as much trouble when he used to do it by himself. And God forbid that I should offer any improvements. The one time I suggested we buy a bouquet of rubber petunias that would last through the winter he glared at me like I had proposed digging up Grandmother's carcass and selling it as dog food. So we continued as before. I rolled him to the grave and arranged the floral tribute, then dawdled among the monuments for however long it took him to suck up enough guilt, grief, and morbidity to last him through the week.

I don't think this graveyard cult would have gotten so advanced if it hadn't been for a certain inferiority Father felt with regard to Mother's relations. In fact, I'm convinced the only reason Father dragged Grandmother's corpse down here in the first place was to compete with the legions of skeletons fertilizing the cemetery from Mother's side of the family. His people were from the hills and found our swamps too malarial for their tastes, so while the town was literally crawling with Mother's kin there was not a single representative of his own bloodline around. Of course he could have remedied this situation by bringing Grandmother down here to stay with us while she was still living, but the truth is that when she was alive he couldn't stand her any more than the rest of us. In Dad's defense I will say this, that in erecting Grandmother's marker at least he didn't go to the insane expense Mother's people did to show off their graves. Obelisks, globes, angels, no whim of vainglory was too vainglorious for that spendthrift crowd. Until he was stopped Uncle Barnett was planning to spend eight thousand dollars on a gaudy mausoleum the size of a granary. The architect had drawn up the plans and was ready to start construction when the town council prohibited it on hygienic grounds. There was concern about a possible problem with odors and the resulting attraction his fragrant remains might hold for vermin.

I guess I felt sorry for my father, because I gave in and agreed to give Quincy a try. After two semesters spent taking Accounting and Business English, where I learned hundreds of useless (to me) commercial abbreviations like whsle., mdse., hhd., flcp., and fwd., wrote full-length treatises on such topics as "Troublesome Plurals," and was subjected to innumerable lectures from the onerous Mr. Stevens—a mustachioed little martinet of a teacher who had a horror of ink blots and who could make the writing of a simple business letter a nightmare—about what a bad impression mouth breathing can produce on the person you're speaking to, I quit. My heart wasn't in it. I told Dad I couldn't take it, and he relented. By this time he was sinking pretty fast. Things didn't have the same importance to him any more. He told me I could go to the university if I wanted, and that's what I did. I read about Genghis Khan making thirty-foot-tall towers out of the severed heads of his vanquished foes. I read about Cortez and his men escaping from Tenochtitlán at night, fighting their way along the causeway, watching the sun sink down behind the top of the pyramid where the Aztecs had tied down their Spanish comrades in order to cut their chests open with obsidian blades and lift their hearts out in sacrificial offerings to their bloodthirsty god Huitzilopochtli and his equally fond-of-gore brother Tezcatlipoca. In the middle of the second year, when Dad died, I went back home for the funeral and then set off for Crete, to see King Minos's Palace and the Labyrinth of the Minotaur and the bare-breasted Snake Goddess whose religious rites included holding adders in both upraised arms while her assistants completed the spectacle by grabbing onto and somersaulting over the razor-sharp horns of huge sacerdotal bulls.

By that time Sarah and I had been history for a long time already. In fact things came to an end soon after I woke up from my quasi-coma, when she came by the house to see me. I was prepared to throw myself at her feet, to bare my soul and unburden my heart with all of the emotion I had been rehearsing at the ice plant, but before I could even begin telling her how sorry I was and pledge my undying loyalty and affection for at least another six months and agree to announce our engagement if she absolutely needed to have it done, she dropped the bombshell on me that she didn't want to hear any of it, that as far as she was concerned it was all over between us, that she'd never been so humiliated in her life. She went on to say that even before this public display of my perfidy she'd already been having second thoughts. She said working with Arlene Pilcher all summer at her parents' restaurant had begun to open her eyes to some truths about the state of marriage. (Arlene had been married for thirty-four years and claimed she still had to wear a girdle to bed at night to keep her husband off her. When her working days were over and she had the time she said she was going to write two books, one called *I Married a Pervert* and the other titled *Ten Thousand Ways to Say No!*) Sarah said the recent events had altered her opinion about the wisdom of getting married so young, and now she not only didn't want anything more to do with me, she didn't care if she ever married anybody at all. Of course this wasn't true, it was just her reaction to the heartache I had caused her, because inside of a year Sarah was engaged and married to none other than that little prick Calvin Lucas who, and he deserves some credit for his timely display of initiative, had taken advantage of my absence at the Passion Play to occupy the empty seat next to Sarah. For the next hour the two of them discovered they shared a common sense of outrage at the drunken debacle unfolding before their eyes. In addition to the revulsion they both felt for the appalling deterioration in the public morals they were witnessing, they found other points of agreement, and by the time they had left the auditorium and split a milkshake at the drugstore, Sarah's anger with me for my inattentiveness of the past few months and her disgust with me for my participation as a seller of intoxicants in the night's affront to religion and morality combined to hasten a definitive shift in her heart's allegiance in the direction of Calvin, who no one in town doubted had a very promising future as a jeweler ahead of him, assuming he successfully completed his three-month watch repair course, which he did. Calvin and Sarah were married the following June.

Wayne spent that Saturday night locked up in jail, courtesy of Sheriff Gordon, a period long enough for the sedative to wear off. For some reason he didn't come looking for me again, and I sure never went looking for him. I never saw him again after that, because by the time I was ambulatory Rachel and Wayne had already left town for a place in Kentucky where Wayne's brother owned a fishing boat and where Wayne presumably would soon find it necessary to beat some other foolhardy adventurer half to death. I'd like to be able to say I didn't have any regrets about the affair, but I had many, among them a place on the side of my skull where the tip of Wayne's boot hit home, leaving an indentation that still throbs whenever I spend too many hours squinting in poor light at whatever obscure tome I'm reading late into the night. I saw Rachel one more time, when she returned for her brother's funeral (he burned to death in a caboose fire when the kerosene heater he was refueling exploded), but she was at one end of Main Street with her mother and I was on the other end on the corner talking to Walking Tom, sipping on a half-pint, and I figured that was close enough for us to get to each other. I don't think she even saw me, and that was all right with me.

Matt's father once told me about a family that insisted on putting dozens of toy rubber dogs in the casket with their mother, because she was so attached to her little cocker spaniel and they didn't want her to be lonely for it. It seems like a harmless enough custom, especially when you compare it to many ancient peoples, who used to put real dogs, and slaves, and donkeys, and wives, and viziers—after killing them—into the tombs with the deceased ruler. For Dad all we did was stick a golf ball and his putter in the casket, because he loved the game so much. In his prime, before he became a truncated effigy of himself, he was a scratch golfer. His drives were prodigious, his long irons soared like rockets, and his short irons were feathery soft. I can still see him standing like a colossus in the sand trap, his sand wedge descending, creating an explosion of tiny white crystals that fly into the air and land in the wispy froghair of the green like so many exquisite diamonds.

Dad wanted me to love golf too, so when I was eight years old he took me to the country club to initiate me into the mysteries of the ancient and venerable Sport of Gentlemen. So it was that I found myself one day in the dank atmosphere of the men's dressing room tying the laces on the white patent leather golf shoes Dad had presented me with that very morning. They were huge and unwieldy and stuck out at the end of my spindly ankles like great pontoons. I didn't want to wear them but I didn't say anything because of the strong sense I had that the ritual of the occasion far outweighed any considerations of appearance or comfort, both of which were already severely compromised anyway by the voluminous knickers I was housed in, which billowed in the breeze like a spinnaker and threatened if not for the weight of those massive shoes to pick me up off the surface of the earth and blow me away.

At the first teebox a group of Dad's golfing cronies, Mr. Randolph the banker, Mr. Bowers who was in insurance, the slicing cattleman Mr. Boyd, and several others, kind men one and all, had gathered to watch the fledgling take wing. Their scrutiny, though well intentioned, made me nervous and doubting of my ability, a doubt which was well-founded considering that my total experience to this point consisted of having under Dad's watchful eye struck about a hundred balls into the cow pasture with a mashie the day before. From that session it was evident that my swing was stiff and mechanical and that having no confidence in the natural arc of the arms and shoulders my tendency was to compensate by lunging at the ball as though trying to disembowel the earth it sat on. Dad wasn't concerned. He assured me that this energy when properly channeled would result in the development of the relaxed and smooth stroke the game requires.

When the moment came for me to tee off I rummaged in my golf bag, which was jammed to bursting with all the strange implements of the game, and pulled out the trusty mashie I had used the day before. But quickly I learned that one does not use one's mashie off the tee. It might do for a shot from fairway to green or off the tee of a medium-length par-three, but on this first monster of a hole, four hundred and fifty yards long if it was a day, and a dogleg or two thrown in, no, if one cannot yet handle the driver one at the very least must propel the sphere with a spoon, which though unaware of the existence of such a thing I in fact possessed. It looked evil, this long black spoon, as it was put into my sweating hands, and I felt it boded ill for me. Nevertheless I took my stance, somewhat precariously in the unfamiliar spikes, and tried to steady myself for the blow I was to deliver. The sunlight was blinding. To my watering eyes the extreme whiteness of the ball made it shimmer and dance like a desert mirage, conjuring images of sidewinding rattlesnakes, alkali pools, and the sun-bleached skulls of pioneer cattle. Off in the distance I could hear crows cawing, the sound becoming fainter and fainter as they flew west toward the cornfields. I wished that I were in flight with them, far above the earth and its demands. But I wasn't. I was holding a golf club on the first tee, in the company of a group of quiet middle-aged men, and even the knowledge that they were silently rooting for me was of no comfort. I was the one who had to swing the club. The moment demanded action, so I began my backswing nervously, awkwardly, forgetting everything my father had told me about drawing the clubhead back skimming the ground in a wide, smooth arc. No, I reared up with the motion of a spastic woodcutter. When I reached the very limit of my arms' length I paused, lacking any feeling of connection between myself and the ground, lost in time and space, in hopeless alienation from my surroundings. With nothing else to do but reverse the motion I had so faultily begun, I descended upon the ball with a desperation equaled only by my lack of proper aim, in a stroke that caused the head of the club to smash into the ground a good foot and a half behind the ball, bounce up and, along with the long black shaft, wholly leave my grasp. This newly launched ensemble flew unerringly toward Mr. Finley, a successful grocer, who wasn't paying attention to my travails at all but had his eyes glued on the eight beautifully tanned legs of a ladies' foursome that was just finishing their round on the eighteenth green. Probably all his life Mr. Finley had wished he was taller than the five feet three inches God had blessed him with, but on this day it was his extreme good fortune to be such a short little man, because it meant he received from the missile that flew from my hands only a rude and violent shock to his stomach, which was of ample proportions and could easily withstand such a concussion, instead of what for a taller man would have been a nasty and debilitating blow to the balls.

Despite this inauspicious beginning, and though it turned out that I had little aptitude for the game, I didn't give it up. With Dad urging me on I chewed up both fairway and green, sending great clods into the air, destroying carefully sodded aprons, emptying sand traps at an alarming rate. I played entire holes by way of the ditches and forests that bounded them, scattering frogs and snakes with my futile swings. And if I have one regret it is that I never became proficient at this sport, a feat that would have been no small source of pride to Dad. But I am grateful for his efforts, because if not for him to this day I would still not know a baffy from a brassie, and I would be subject to the cruel humiliations life vents upon the ignorant.

La Bulime

Act I

In a drab chambre de bonne in Paris, Rodolfo, poète-maudit of
the Latin Quarter, and his friend Marcello, a pornographic crock-
ery sculptor, are high on Robitussin and airplane glue. They are
burning their downstairs landlord's clothes for fuel because he has
departed en vacances and left them heatless. Their friends Colline,
a student-philosopher devoted to making Esperanto the international tongue, and Schumber, who sings in the subways, arrive with
pants bulging with baguettes stolen from the blind pâtissier on Rue
Jacob. They feast. Their merriment is interrupted by their personal
hashish dealer who arrives with a bill for 7,000 new francs, threatening to have their eyes and tongues removed if they don't pay.
This weak-willed individual, who will soon be found floating in
the Seine, done in by his friends of the demimonde, winds up shar-
ing the six grams he has with him. They all get stoned and leave,
except for Rodolfo and the dealer. The dealer passes out and
Rodolfo has started going through his pockets when there is a
knock on the door. Rodolfo shoves the dealer onto the roof and
closes the dormer window. He opens the door to find Mimi, an
excruciatingly thin yet oddly attractive young lady, gnawing on a
turkey leg. She asks if she can borrow some mayonnaise. Rodolfo
admits her to the room and while he is looking inside the fridge
she opens the dormer window, gags herself, and vomits on the unseen and unconscious dealer. Quickly she closes the window and
resumes eating as Rodolfo enumerates the contents of the refrig-

erator: olives, herring, half a blood sausage. She says these will do. Rodolfo brings the food out and they share a meal. Rodolfo lights up his hash pipe, Mimi eats, they talk. They quickly reach a deep level of understanding, discovering they both come from dysfunctional families with cold mothers and authoritarian fathers with alcoholic tendencies. Each dreams of finding a life-partner they can abuse, at least until the winter is over, because in the spring their disgust for themselves and the world reaches such a height that they dispose of any relationship in which they are involved in as messy and damaging a way as possible in order to enter a new period of intense guilt and self-reproach. As their rapture heightens, Rodolfo hears his friends calling to him from outside and answers that he will join them with his new friend, Mimi. They embrace, Mimi stashes the jar of olives in her purse, and they leave for the café arm in arm.

Act II

Using the money from the dealer's pockets, Rodolfo finances an eating binge by Mimi, who downs popcorn, taco chips, sugar cookies, a corndog, cotton candy, two bags of pork rinds, and a dozen cupcakes. When they meet Rodolfo's friends on the street Mimi turns aside as if to buy a newspaper, puts a franc in the machine, gags herself, and vomits into the newspaper dispenser. A condom vendor with his colorful cart comes by followed by a gaggle of clamoring twelve-year-olds waving hundred-franc notes. Rodolfo and Mimi enter the café, where she is introduced to his friends. Soon a limousine pulls up and disgorges Musetta, a pre-op transvestite with enormous bosoms and a deep husky voice. Formerly Marcello's lover, now she has found a rich investment banker who dotes on her and loves to have her tie a string around his penis like a noose and pull it until the circulation is cut off. Musetta, in platform heels, leaps on a table, removes her top, and shakes her tits at anyone who will watch, and in her rich baritone she sings about the vast numbers of stockbrokers and real estate magnates who are vying for her favors. There is A., who likes to wear diapers and be called Sissy-Boy and have her scold him for pissing in his pants. There is B., who likes to pretend to murder her with a machine gun as she feigns recoiling, jerking her body in staccato action to the whumpwhumpwhump tackatackatacka of the bullets. And C., the rarest of all, who wears baby girl dresses and a tutu and begs her to allow him to taste just the slightest morsel of her fecal matter on a slice of whole wheat toast. She brags that it will cost him much more if he wants to obtain this greatest gift. Musetta gets down from the table, sends her banker off on an errand to find more pre-op revelers for a party, then falls into Marcello's arms. When the waiter arrives with the bill they slap him down to the floor and all run out to a waiting cab.

Act III

Winter. Mimi enters the stage, searching for the neighborhood cocaine den. She is now a cruiserweight, tipping the scales at one hundred and ninety pounds. Her underwear size has grown from 4 to 18 in one act. She is feeding on a live grouse she has netted in the park, her teeth ripping into its flesh and drinking the blood as it runs down her chin. Marcello emerges from the drug house. Mimi tells him that she's going to leave Rodolfo. He isn't supporting her as he should. She is in Overeaters Anonymous, Debtors Anonymous, Alcoholics Anonymous, Narcotics Anonymous, Adult Children of Alcoholics Anonymous, Fundamentalists Anonymous, and Sexaholics Anonymous. Rodolfo is in denial. He is still drinking Robitussin. He says he can quit whenever he wants to, he just doesn't want to. He drinks, broods, wants her to stay away from her meetings. Rodolfo emerges from the cocaine den. Mimi hides behind the bushes. Rodolfo sees Marcello and tells him he wants to leave Mimi. "I'm bored to death, plus she's fat," he says. "I liked her better when she was vomiting." Then he breaks down and says he knows Mimi is doomed. Her blood pressure is 220 over 150. There is a bad family history of infarctus and aneurysm. Since she quit smoking their life has been a nightmare. She eats butterscotch and peppermint candies by the bagful. "It's like making love to a convertible sofa," he says. Then he starts crying and says he loves her no matter what. Mimi emerges from the shrubbery with a still-quivering squirrel she has unconsciously been strangling while listening to Rodolfo. Marcello, hearing a fusillade of bullet shots from the drug den, goes inside. Mimi and Rodolfo share their love, Rodolfo pledging to love her until the next procession of the equinox, if only she'll stop hounding him about the twelve-step meetings. Mimi, deep in the middle of a major slip in almost every category, agrees. Chewing on the squirrel leg she looks into Rodolfo's eyes, turns aside to vomit, then kisses him. Marcello runs out of the house with Musetta behind him, bullets flying over their heads.

Act IV

In the garret. Rodolfo and Marcello are smoking crack, shooting up crystal meth, sniffing glue, and taking Ecstasy. Colline and Schumber join them. They stage a mock ball. Musetta bursts in to announce that Mimi is downstairs. She wants the four of them to carry her up the staircase. She weighs about four hundred pounds now and wants to die near Rodolfo. They debate the subject. How will they get rid of the body afterward? It's too late, Mimi has managed to get upstairs, stripping the gears of the ascenseur and crawling the final floor. They put her on the bed, which immediately collapses, its feet going through the floorboards. Musetta goes to the street to give a blow job to get enough money to buy Mimi a pastrami hoagie. Mimi reminds Rodolfo of the happy days when she was vomiting, if only she had kept it up. She tries to gag herself but only manages to belch. Musetta returns. Mimi is eating sugar out of the sugar bowl, chasing it with gobs of organic peanut butter. Suddenly a serene look comes on her face. She pukes and dies. Colline lowers the blinds, Schumber crosses himself, and Rodolfo throws himself on top of Mimi. His wails and piteous sobs fill the room as he surreptitiously ferrets through Mimi's purse to remove her rings and jewelry for later sale to his fence.

CURTAIN

Exit

She lied to me. She said she was in love with me. This was after three weeks of sleeping together. Maybe she believed it. "I'm falling in love with you," she said. We were in bed. We had just made love. It was summer. We'd been making love for three weeks. "I'm falling in love with you, too," I said.

Now she says "I'm not in love with you." She says this late at night when we're in bed together. She starts crying. "I'm not in love with you," she sobs. I don't know what to say so I don't say anything. I think about the past six months: the trip to Canada where we lay on the rocks next to the rust-red water of the Moisie River, watching the salmon congregate in the deep pools; the trip to Pittsburgh to meet her parents, sitting in the den talking about quilts with her mother and golf with her father; the afternoon we spent in Central Park on a blanket under an early autumn sun with the leaves just starting to turn, holding each other and reminiscing, her remembering the first time she got felt up, by David Epstein, walking home from Hebrew School one late afternoon, me recalling the first girl's brassiere I managed to infiltrate, Karen Delaney's, behind a huge magnolia tree at Methodist summer camp. I thought about these moments, these images, and the feelings that went with them, and I said to myself, "That's all down the tubes now."

The next morning I gave her back her umbrella I'd been using. I gave her the extra pair of underwear she kept at my house for when she stayed overnight. I gave her all the photographs from Quebec, Pittsburgh, and Central Park. "I don't want these around," I said. We said good-bye at the door. She was crying. "I love you," she said. I didn't say anything. She turned and left. She didn't look back.

Willie and Jackie

Willie the Wildebeest roamed the veldt, knock-kneed and clumsy, accidentally kicking over termite towers and crushing vole burrows, hearing the screams of marauding cheetahs in the night, trembling a bit in his sleep, lonely and alone, missing all the things that make life worth living—comradery, wit, laughter, romance—wishing he had someone pretty, someone female to share his cud with.

Jackie the Jellyfish floated on the ocean, buffeted by sea swells and the wakes of passing freighters, thinking to herself as she paralyzed another smelt with her tentacles and slowly drew it up into her mouth to be digested, "There must be more to life than this." She, too, was alone, drifting far on the fringes of the current that swept her and her kin to and fro from island to atoll, from reef to beach. But somewhere in that diaphanous sphere of plasma there beat a heart, and inside that heart was a soul that longed for companionship, for friendship, for, in a word, love.

One day Willie caught a scent of something in the air, a seabreeze, a tinge of salt, that he felt drawing him westward across the savannah, through the Kalahari, along gulches and dry river washes, past hippo wallows and over the high plains speckled with baobab trees. Westward it drew him, unconsciously, since he didn't know he was going west, he didn't know he smelled salt, he just knew that he was impelled toward something that an animal with a less sensitive olfactory bulb but a higher understanding might call destiny.

In the ocean a similar tug was being felt by Jackie, to the extent a jellyfish can be said to feel. The tug seemed to pull Jackie contrary to the usual currents, and for the first time in her life she struggled, she strived instead of being content to float along with the current. Her efforts seemed to bear her toward land, eastward, a direction she had never been before unless a typhoon or tropical depression willed it, and then it wasn't so much a direction as a rout of wind and foam that blew her brains so dizzy she didn't know where she was. Eastward, eastward, with increasing speed, a peculiar smell in her . . . nostrils? . . . no, in her being. She felt the smell of soil, of land and of vegetation that grew out of solid ground.

Westward and eastward they plunged on, one kicking hyenas off his heels and scattering fang-baring baboons from a water hole, the other electrocuting curious remoras and amorous squids, each of them intent on something they couldn't even begin to define or comprehend.

Finally they reached their common destination, a beach, with diamond sparkling sand and blue crashing breakers, and the sky as big and wide as the soul of God towering above them. The air was sweet with the smell of expectation and longing. But just at the moment when Willie thought he caught a glimpse of something that looked like a beautiful pearl balloon bobbing in the waves, and just as Jackie "saw" a gangly moth-riddled shag carpet on stilts just above the crest of the wave she was riding, the Namibian beach patrol—four drunken louts firing M-16 carbines into the air while gulping the worst piss-tasting beer you can imagine—ran smack into Willie, rending him limb from limb and sending big gouts of wildebeest blood spurting into the air. And out in the surf a shore surveillance team came roaring along in their one-hundred horsepower outboard whose propeller chopped Jackie up into one million little pieces, leaving only tiny specks of matter that took hours to waft down to the mouths of the various bottom-feeding species that inhabit the coastal waters off the West African mainland.

Such, then, was Willie and Jackie's moment of love.

It was not, of course, without issue. Nothing ever is. Willie's flesh and bones, tanned and scoured by the sun and by turkey hawks and vultures, and Jackie's iridescent particles, eaten and eliminated by other sea-dwelling creatures, mingled there in the surf of the Great Continent and were gradually reabsorbed into the Wheel of Life, bound to be spit out again some day into two new distinct and disparate forms. A tangerine and a tomato perhaps. Or a flea and a ferret. Or a crow and a caterpillar. And then one day the great yearning will arise again, deep within the cells something will stir, somewhere else something will respond, and the power of love—irresistible, mysterious, all-healing—will bring the two lovers together once more, as one, all over the earth, until the end of time.

The Diary of Oedipus

Monday, July 7

Fucked Mom again today. Afterward felt satisfied but ashamed. It's that little voice of guilt that I hear sometimes. My shrink says to ignore it, it's just that old negative tape running in my head that tells me I don't deserve the good things in life. Mom doesn't seem to have any idea that we're related. That's good because if she knew she'd have a cow. Maybe that's what has me on edge a little. There've been some things in the paper lately, some blind items in Tiresias's column alluding to some improprieties in a socially prominent family. Like last week: "What would people say if the relations between a certain 'Rex' (and I don't mean Rex the Wonder Dog) and his current sweetheart were found to be closer than anyone can imagine? If we could only tell everything we know! But then, darlings, you wouldn't have any reason to keep reading my scribblings. Stay tuned." That bastard. Newspaper whore. Why doesn't he write about the banker from St. Louis whose knob he's been polishing to pay for his boob job? I'll get Judge Krater to see what it'll take to buy him off. Little boys no doubt. There're plenty of those around. Anyway, Mom and I are doing fine. I'm glad Dad is dead.

Wednesday, July 9

Played golf today. Rode in the cart because my foot was hurting me. It really swells up in the summer. The doctor says it's my

Achilles tendon (it really should be named after me. I had it long before that little swish came along). Still I was four under through seven holes until I hit the water on number eight. Then the whole thing unraveled. I shanked my drive on nine, was in the sand on ten, finally quit on thirteen, and went to the clubhouse and had a few drinks. I saw Vernon there. The drought is really bad out his way. The corn is burning up. Wells are dry. Says he'll be lucky to make ten bushels an acre. Forget the soybeans and wheat, they didn't even come up. He wants me to get Representative Caldwell down here. Not much of a chance of that until he gets out of detox. He's got ten more days in Hazelden. Vernon said, "You're the mayor here. Can't you do anything?"

Thursday, July 10

Had that dream again last night. The one where I'm killing Dad. I really beat him to a bloody pulp. Hell, I didn't even know he was my father at the time. If I had, I would have cut his dick off, too. I mean face it, the man tried to do me harm. I've got the scars to prove it. And he didn't serve one day of time. If you can't do the time, don't do the crime. That was my campaign slogan. Law and order. Justice was served, in my opinion. Tiresias thinks he's on to something. Today he wrote "An old murder case that shocked this community ten years ago is heating up with new leads pointing to someone whose nouveau prominence has been a source of annoyance to many." In another place in his column he called me a do-nothing. What does he want me to do? A rain dance? All we need is a couple of thundershowers and everything'll turn green again.

Friday, July 11

Had a little scene with Mom today. I complained about her putting on cold cream before we go to bed and she burst into tears. "I know I make you feel old," she said. "You'll leave me for some young girl who drives a convertible and plays beach volleyball." Her intuition is amazing. It's almost like she knew I went out with Georgianne last week. I like Georgianne a lot. She's nice. She's crazy about me and I'm just crazy, ha ha ha. But it bothered me when she said, "What do you see in that old hag anyway." It was a pretty annoying thing to say and I let her know it. I told her I didn't want to see her again. Now she knows she went too far and is falling all over herself apologizing. I'll probably call her this weekend. She wears the most enchanting perfume. Great legs, too, and nice tits. It's worth checking out again. But I'd never give up my mother for her.

Monday, July 14

Citizens committee meeting today. It was unbelievable. One after another jumped up and gave me shit. On TV, too. Channel 4 from Beardonsville came down to the community center. Ted Miller said, "You're the cause of all this. What are you going to do about it?" Ed Glidden said I should resign. There was talk about a recall petition. Tiresias started asking about my birth certificate. He said no one could seem to find it. "Has your name always been Oedipus?" he said. There's a good reason no one can find it. I had Krater get rid of it a long time ago. It's off the records. I didn't want that piece of hot news lying around the Department of Natural Statistics office for any old snoop to find.

The Diary of Oedipus

Wednesday, July 16

Sometimes I'm sorry I killed Dad. I never had a father except for that old fuck Lester. Stupid farmer bored me to death. Talking about god, religion, philosophy. Reciting Homer to me day and night. Another blind jerk. What's going on? It's not like we have African river blindness around here. People think blindness equals wisdom. Well what about old Blind Fred back in Corinth? He was the most ill-tempered asshole I ever knew. He hated everybody. You could hear him screaming at his wife and kids from a block away. I used to leave my bicycle lying on the sidewalk to trip him up when he came by with his cart full of brooms he was taking downtown to sell. He always found it with his cane and tapped his way around it. The fat fuck. He deserved to fall flat on his face.

Saturday, July 19

Mom's getting suspicious. She was quizzing me this morning. Asked a lot of questions about what I did before I moved here. I told her we'd been through all that before. She especially wanted to know about the vehicular homicide rap I beat. Who was it I killed? What did he look like? How old was he? I told her "Look, it was night, it was dark, it was an old drunk stumbling in the middle of a fork in the road. I couldn't stop in time and all four wheels ran him over." (I didn't tell her that after I ran over him once I backed up and ran over him again to make sure of the job.) When I asked her why she was so curious she said it was because she's worried my political enemies will use it against me. I told her to stop worrying, it's not like I drove my car off a bridge and drowned a blond in ten feet of water. I'm clean as a whistle on this one. No one can touch me. But I'm going to find out who's been filling her head with stories.

Monday, July 21

The shit is about to hit the fan. Tiresias has called a news conference. He's talking about bringing in an outside prosecutor. He's got Jake Creon, the police chief on his side. That backstabber. I let him sell insurance to the city, got him a new squad car, and came up with the funds for a new interrogation room, and this is how he treats me! If he thinks I'm going to sit idly by and let him make me the first person he interrogates in there he's got another think coming. That's not going to happen. I'll leave the fucking country before I let those jackals at me.

Wednesday, July 23

Did a stupid thing today. I put my eyes out with knitting needles. I just lost my head. I guess it was seeing Mom hanging from the rafters that set me off. It's all that Tiresias's fault. His accusations, his columns, his snide comments. Mom finally put two and two together, ran into the house, and hung herself. Who's going to take care of the kids now? I probably should have done the same thing, but after seeing her bulging eyes and blue lips I was too much of a coward. I just grabbed the knitting needles and rammed them home. Now I'm in a fix. At least it's gained me some time. They haven't impeached me. If they do, I'll run again. I might get the sympathy vote. If worst comes to worst I might have to get out of town. But I'm ready for that. I've got two tickets to Brazil in my pocket. I bought two, for Mom and me, but now I guess I'll see if Georgianne will go. If not, the hell with it, I'll find somebody. I'll be all right, even blind. I'll get a three-legged seeing-eye dog. It's a great way to pick up women. Everyone is interested in a three-legged dog. A friend of mine took one to Myrtle Beach and the girls wouldn't leave him alone.

The Diary of Oedipus

Thursday, July 24

It's over. Creon's won. He and Tiresias are in power now. Let them have the stinking place! Six months under him and people will be begging for me to come back. He's not a bad administrator, but he's so self-righteous. He acts like no one ever screwed around before. He's probably impotent. Or maybe he and Tiresias have a thing going. Fuck 'em both. They won't have Oedipus to kick around anymore. But my career isn't over, not by a long shot. I'll leave this shithole and go someplace where people appreciate a man who can kill a Sphinx just by answering a riddle. I'll establish a power base, run for office, make it all the way back. The kids can come visit on weekends.

Friday, July 25. Highway 3, in a car leaving Thebes, Illinois

This is it. Leaving the old hometown, maybe forever. Lots of memories, lots of good times. My driver is an old black man who won't go faster than forty-five. I can hear the semis blaring their horns at him to speed up. I told him to give it the juice, but he won't do it. Must be a line of traffic a mile long behind us. No place to pass on this winding little road. So this is what it's like to be blind. It's not so bad. I don't have to worry about anything. I've got my pension. Some real estate—those lots where the new highway is going to go through. A shoebox full of cash. Public office can pay off if you know how to use it. Now that I can't see I guess I'll get a reputation for being pretty shrewd. It's amazing what a pair of shades and a cane can do for your image. When the kids are old enough I'll tell 'em the whole story. They'll die when they find out. They won't believe it. Forty miles to Carbondale. At this rate it'll take us an hour to get there, so I think I'll take a little snooze. So long, suckers. I'm out of here.

The Pink Clouds Are Blood

This is how I grieved for you:
I went to India
I wrote fifteen stories
I fell in love
I got a kidney infection
I went to Brazil
I wanted to kill myself
I bought flowers
I moved
I bought new clothes
I saved everything from the hospital
I got out of shape
I got into shape
I had three more girlfriends
I carried your ashes to Canada
I spent Memorial Day in bed
I missed you
I didn't miss you
I started smoking
I hated myself
I got a great tan
I got lonely
I played basketball
I went somewhere every month
I put your paintings on my wall

The Pink Clouds Are Blood

I saw you everywhere
I saw your hair
Your belt
Your sunglasses
I looked at the sky at dusk
The clouds were pink and gray
You were nowhere on the earth